Let Sleeping Dogs Lie

DEDICATION

To my biggest, fan Carolyn Hawthorn (mom), thank you for your support, interest, and encouragement. I love you, dearly, admire, and respect all that you have gone through to raise us on your own. Sorry, it so long to get this one out there. I know you've been waiting for it.

Always in my heart Corrine Helen Marrioneaux, Larry (Joseph Peter) Miller, Jules Jenkins, and the person's whose personality I include in most of my stories, Antoinette Drayton Damron, without your eccentric personality, I don't think I would be able to come up with an antagonist personality.

CONTENTS

	Dedication	i
1	Guarded Secrets	Pg.1
2	Dream Terror	Pg. 10
3	Evil Lurks	Pg. 25
4	WTF Happened	Pg. 45
5	Evil Is...	Pg. 58
6	Nobody's Perfect	Pg. 86
7	Evil Does...	Pg. 101
8	Enemy of my Enemy	Pg. 114
9	Opportunity Knocks	Pg. 135
10	Meeting of the Minds	Pg. 147
11	Enough is Enough	Pg. 164
12	Every Dog has it's Day	Pg. 177

GUARDED SECRET

It is a cool bright Saturday afternoon, with winds blowing autumn leaves around the house and on to the large wrap around porch of Chelsea Webber's Victorian style house. The coolness of the breezes brings the aroma of fresh cut grass and a hint of the Lavender from the field across the street. The breezes that blow across her face and through her hair makes her feel embraced by the wind. She lays her head back on the porch swing and closes her eyes. She reminisces back to when she was a child of eight when she, her brother Larry and his best friend Timothy were at an empty baseball diamond catching bees and grasshoppers in jars.

As clear as the day it happened, she sees her brother and Timmy a little distance away from her and shortly after she hears the sound of Larry's voice calling her name.

"Chelsea, why don't you catch the bees instead of those boring grasshoppers? The bees make it more daring."

"She's scared she's going to get stung." Timmy chuckled. *"Chelsea is a fraidy-cat!"* He teased. Then without warning, Timmy runs off screaming, holding his buttocks. Her brother stood bent over, laughing so hard at the sight of

Timmy getting a bee sting on the butt. She couldn't help but laugh with him and thinking... *"He shouldn't have been teasing me."*

    A telephone ringing in the background brings her back to the present. She goes to answer the phone, still smiling a little at the sight of Timmy running home with his hand over his butt that day.

The sun light beams through, white lacy sheers that hang snuggled between emerald green draperies shadows the living room as she walks in from the porch.

    "Hello." She answers the phone.

    "Hey Chels, I was just calling to see if you were doing anything later this afternoon?" the caller asks.

    "Well, actually, I would love the company if you would like to come over for a while."

    "Sure! I'll stop and rent a couple of movies and pick up something for dinner."

Almost as instant as Chelsea replies, she remembers that she already has a dinner guest for the evening but, the invitation is now out there, and she can't take it back without having to explain. Although, after successfully leaving her abusive husband Harris Foster, she and Brooklyn made a solemn promise to each other, never to allow anyone or anything to come between their friendship.

    "That's fine, Brook. What time do you think

you'll get here?" She asks, looking at her watch.
"I'll leave in about thirty minutes or so."
"Alright, see you soon." She says before hanging up the phone.

Chelsea is washing dishes from lunch as she gazes out the kitchen window at the colorful sunset while talking to Ronald on the phone. The kitchen window displays the view of the large back yard, furnished with a gazebo, and an old empty well that Chelsea's great-grandfather installed at the time he built the house back in the 1800s. Pink and white roses grow around the gazebo using its structure for support during their growing periods. The doorbell rings.

"I'm sorry to have to cancel our plans. Will you take a rain check?" She explains.

"That's fine babe, just give me a ring tomorrow." He replies.

"Okay. I have to go; someone is at the door."

*

She wishes so much that it was Ronald at the door instead of Brooklyn. Then again, she felt a little guilty for even thinking that way. Maybe tonight would be an excellent opportunity for her to talk about her involvement with him but, Brooklyn has a way with, throwing her abusive marriage up in her face, and that's the last thing she wants to hear; especially since she's no longer with him.

She peeks out the window behind the sofa as Brooklyn parks her car behind her minivan.

"Hey! What did you bring for dinner?" Chelsea greets as she opens the door.

"Well, we have shrimp gumbo, and for dessert, we have Jamoca Almond fudge ice cream." She replies, walking towards the kitchen.

"Mmm, that sounds good, especially since we don't have to cook it."

"Well, you do have a part in this, you know." Brooklyn says.

"What?"

"You can at least serve the meal, thank you."

"Is that all? No problem."

"Oh, Chelsea! I've got something juicy to tell you!"

"What? What happened?"

"Do you remember Morgan Couch?"

"How could I forget, aside from the fact that he is extremely handsome, and you're constantly talking about him...what about him?"

"We did it!"

"Did what?"

"You know very well, what."

"Well, it's about time. How was he?"

"He was so sweet." Brooklyn glows. "We went out yesterday for lunch, and then after the movies last night, we went back to his apartment, where I stayed the night."

"Well, ...was he everything you thought he would be?"

"Oh, yes!" She answers with a flushed face.

"He must have been. Your rosy smile almost tells it all." Chelsea says, munching on potato chips.

She gets the dishes ready for their dinner, while Brooklyn is in the dining room clearing away the fine china from the table when there is a knock at the door.

"Brook, can you get the door for me, please?" Chelsea calls from the kitchen.

Brooklyn returns from the door holding a flower box in her arm.

"Who was it?"

"A delivery person."

"Oh, flowers! Did you tell Morgan you were going to be here?"

"No," she answers, pulling a small pink card from beneath the ribbon. "But who is Ron?"

Surprised more than she leads on to be, Chelsea quickly takes the card away and reads it silently. The card reads; *"I hope you believe that I'm not angry with you and still look forward to seeing you again."*

"Ron is a friend from work that's interested in me." She answers with a smile and takes the box of flowers to the kitchen. She smiles with uncertainty, not knowing if Brooklyn is going to lecture her on getting into a relationship so soon.

"So, you've been holding out on me...but why?" Brooklyn asks.

"You lectured me for so long on getting back into a relationship, I just didn't want to hear it anymore. I was going to tell you about him."

"Well, now, you have to."

"What do you want to know?"

"The basics...age, career, and more importantly, how long have you been seeing him?"

"Ron is the CPA in the office building I work at. We have been seeing each other for a year now. He's thirty-seven, never been married, and has no children."

"I'm so happy for you and at the same time a little hurt that you felt you couldn't tell me. I didn't realize that I was that hard on you, and I'm sorry."

"No need to apologize. I'm sincerely grateful for your concern for me. You're the only one I have left in my life that knows where I am and makes me feel at home. I'm sorry that I didn't tell you."

"When are you going to let me meet him?"

"Soon, I'm sure. We're supposed to set something up soon, but I'm not sure when."

"Hey! We could double date! Dinner and a

movie and maybe come back for a game of cards."

"We'll see, Brook." Chelsea smiles.

After dinner, they sit in the living room playing cards with the television on until Chelsea begins to feel sleepy but, the entire time, Ron is still running through her mind, and occasionally Brooklyn would catch her smiling for no reason.

Losing the game royally to Brooklyn due to her lack of attention to the game, she is ready to hang it up for the evening.

"Brook, this is my last hand, and then I'm going to take a shower and hit the sack. I can hardly keep my eyes open, I'm so sleepy."

"Yeah, yeah, you're just sore because you're losing." She teases.

"Whatever... I just know that when my head hits that pillow, I'm going to let the sandman take me away."

"Gin, I win!" Brooklyn shouted in glory.

"Good. Now I'm going to take my shower." Chelsea says, placing her cards on the remaining deck.

**

Brooklyn always thought it was odd that Chelsea had the guest room in the front of the house off the living room and not upstairs. From the time, Chelsea moved into the house, Brooklyn would always tell her that the room should be a den or an office and not a guest room. Instead, Chelsea tells her that she prefers to have her office upstairs near her bedroom...then too, Brooklyn thought it odd that she kept that door under lock and key.

    Even on rare occasions that Chelsea has gone up there with Brooklyn visiting, she would still lock the door from the inside. Whenever Brooklyn would ask if she could see how she had her office set up, she would always come up with an excuse or lame reason for why she couldn't and insisted that she would like her to stop asking and let her have her privacy. They have had a few heated arguments about what is upstairs because, Brooklyn didn't want to accept that she didn't have anything to hide and, if it were any other room it wouldn't have been a big deal.

    Eventually, Chelsea was able to persuade her to see her point of view as far as her privacy, by recalling how her husband Harris demanded to know everything; including her whereabouts after work. It was so bad that he had ruined almost every gift she tried to surprise him with. Brooklyn has not asked since, but her curiosity is still there because even now when she makes the trip up there, she still locks the door once she's on the other side.

*

After Brooklyn has her shower and is dressed

for bed, she looks at the clock and sees that it is just ten forty-five and, she is nowhere near sleepy. She goes into Chelsea's room to find out more about her new friend Ron.

"Chels, are you sleep yet?" She asks, standing in the doorway.

"Not quite. You can come in." She replies and sits up in the bed, dozing off while watching television.

"So, tell me more about Ron." She said, plopping down across the foot of her bed.

"There's nothing more to tell."

"Well, how do you feel about him?"

"It's too soon to say. We just really started to go out with each other. Tonight, would have been the first date." She says.

"So, what do you think about double dating until you're comfortable with him."

"I think that's a good idea, but maybe next time."

"Ok. Hey, this is one of my favorite movies. Do you mind if I stay and watch it with you?"

"Sure, why not?" She answers, with her eyes rolling to the back of her head, as her eyelids grow heavier.

NIGHT TERROR

The bathroom light is dimmed by scented candles that sit on the vanity and on the corners of the bathtub. Chelsea carefully examines her face to see if she can find that candlelit beauty her husband often praises. She remembers the way he looked at her last night during the candlelit dinner she prepared for their sixth month anniversary; she catches herself smiling in the mirror as a warm tingle surges through her body. She pulls her shoulder-length hair up into a bun on the top of her head.
As beautiful as she is, she did not come to realize this until her husband pointed out every beautiful part of her body and personality. She is five feet six inches tall and weighs one hundred and forty pounds with a very well proportion figure.

She turns off the bath water and reaches in to test the temperature with her hand. She turns the radio on to a classical station and returns to step into the bath. The heat of the water sends a chill up her body and makes her belly muscles tighten until she's comfortable with the hot temperature. The water is steaming hot, fogging up the bathroom with its lavender aroma of the bubbles. She lies back and closes her eyes to the therapeutic heat of the water. This is the most soothing and relaxing part of her day that she often looks forward to. Moments later, she dozes off into a light slumber.

There is a sudden cool breeze as if someone had come into the bathroom, she opens her eyes but, it's too dark and steamy to see past her hand in front of her.

"Harris? Is that you?" she calls out.
Satisfied that she must be imagining things, she lays back and closes her eyes again. Just as she closes her eyes, she loses her breath and is unable to take another as hands are choking her. She kicks and swings at her assailant and tries to pry the fingers from around her neck but can't seem to get a firm enough grip on them or beneath them. Her head is forced under the water as the choking becomes stronger and tighter. Beating on the arms of the choker does not seem to help at all, as she continues to kick and swing her arms, splashing water all around. For a second, she can no longer see the shadows of the light that shines from the candles, she can no longer hear the splashing around her, nor feel the hands that were around her neck... but she can breathe again.

She is taken out of the water and slammed against the wall with her hands pinned to her back just below her shoulder blades. Screaming with fear and pain, there is an almost familiar deep whisper in her ear.

"Shut up!"

She begins kicking backward in hopes of hurting this person. She runs free when the assailant yells in pain from a kick to the groin. Hearing his heavy breathing and footsteps coming closer, she turns the knob, but it won't open, he's locked it from the inside. Running closely behind her is a tall, muscular man with blue jeans, black leather gloves and a black leather facemask with silver studs on the chin and above the lip area. Still struggling with the lock and door, she screams at the sight of this man moving in on her.

Once again, he grabs her by the neck tightly to silence her cry for help. He reaches into his pocket and pulls out a knife with a jagged edge on one side and a sharp edge on the other. He places the knife up to her face and slowly moves it down to her throat, then to her left nipple. Still holding her by the neck, he warns her that if she screams again, he will cut her throat.

"Get over there on the bed and don't try anything else! Don't ask any questions and don't speak unless I tell you to!" he orders.

Reluctantly, she sits on the edge of the bed. As the assailant releases her neck, he tightly covers her mouth with his left hand to drown out any sound she may attempt to make, then pulls out several nylon straps with his free hand from the inner pocket of his jacket. She begins to fight again but, he quickly pins her to the bed and straddles her torso, and with all his might, he strikes her across the face for her attempt to fight him. While straddling her, he places her arms under his legs and begins to tie her hands together and then to the bedposts. She screams and pleads with him, not to hurt her.

"I said, shut up!" he yells with another slap to her face.

"Please don't hurt me!" She pleads with tears of fear running down her face.

"What did I just tell you?" he demands sternly then, stuffs a nylon strap in her mouth and tying it closed with another strap.

Once she is bound, he moves down and off the bed and looks at her nakedness in admiration. She shivers from cold. He stares into her water-filled eyes and pulls the blankets over her. He walks into the bathroom and returns with a dry towel, lays it down beside her and begins to dry her hair for her. He removes his mask and places his index finger over his lips to indicate her silence. She looks into his eyes with shock and mumbles words of questions.

"I'm going to untie your mouth, and I don't want you to scream; is that understood?"

She nods in favor of his question.

"Harris, what in the hell is wrong with you? Why are you-?" He interrupts with a backhand slap to her face. The pain of the blow brought a muffled scream and more tears from her eyes.

"What did I tell you? Not one word until I say you can speak." He appears to be a complete stranger looking into his eyes is like looking into someone else's. Frightened and confused, Chelsea complies with his demands, because if nothing else, she wants this moment to be explained and over.

"First of all, do not talk to me using profanity or with that tone of voice, because I will make you regret it." He said. "I saw you with that man this afternoon and the way you were looking at him. Every time we're out or around other people, I find you looking at men as if you want them inside you or something, and I don't appreciate that shit! I never did, and I never will. You will not make a fool of me! But I have something for you, just in case you think you may get lucky enough to screw around with someone else."

He reaches for the knife that he laid beside her while he tied her hands to the headposts and tied her feet to the foot posts of the bed. He sits beside her and kisses her mouth, then recovers her mouth to muffle the noise.

"I love you beautiful." He whispered in her ear.

Turning his back towards her and with his left arm on the other side of her, he braced himself so that she will not see what he is about to do to her. She feels the warmth of his breath on her pubic area as he kissed just above the hairline.

"Aaaaahhhhh!" She screams herself awake.
Her hands are trembling, and her nightgown is wet with sweat, yet she is not hot. She stumbles out of bed on the way to the bathroom and turns on the light. She turns on the water, and as the water runs, she looks at herself in the mirror and sees how soaked her hair and gown is. Cupping her hands together, she captures the water and splashes it on her face, feeling somewhat relieved that it was all just another nightmare of her past. As she prepares to leave, she catches a glimpse of her reflection and notices fresh blood on her gown near her abdomen. She pulls her gown up and finds a cut. Rubbing away the blood, she reveals the letter "H" engraved in her skin. Looking up in disbelief, she slowly backs out of the bathroom staring at her pale skin, as her eyes appear to be completely black.

Still taking small steps out of the bathroom and crying, her appearance in the mirror becomes further and further away as the light casts her shadow upon the floor behind her. Again, she looks at her bloody hands and tries to wipe it away on her gown as she continues to back into the bedroom. As she turns to run out, she bumps into the arms of Harris.

"Chelsea." *He calls to her, with an in his eyes. She can feel the warmth of his breath on her neck as he whispers,* "I love you, Chelsea," *in her ear.*

"Nooo!" *she cries.* "Please, no more! Please

don't. Nooo!"

"Chels, honey, wake up! You're just having a nightmare!" Brooklyn tries to comfort.
Chelsea wakes confused with a sudden jerk, a pounding heart, and trembling body. She feels the hands on her arm gently shaking her and the warmth of the body beside her. She slowly turns to see who is in bed with her in the dark room, she can only see a shadow of a person; arousing her fear once again; she screams, kicks and swings her hands and fists.

"Chelsea, stop it! You're dreaming honey. Wake up!" Brooklyn shakes her harder to wake her. Slowly she becomes aware of her surroundings and the familiar face of her best friend. She put her face in her hands and began to cry, hoping Harris will never find her, never be able to cause her any harm again. She sits on the edge of the bed and begins examining her gown for blood, but it is too dark in the room. She stands with trembling knees; barely able to keep her balance, as she walks to the bathroom.

"Chels, are you alright?"

"Yes; you should go back to sleep. I'm fine."

"Alright, but don't feel bad about waking me if you need to talk or something."

"Thanks, but I'm okay." She replies, closing the bathroom door behind her as she turns on the light.

As she adjusts her eyes to the light, she quickly

splashes cool water on her face. She stares at her wet, frightened face in the mirror and remembers the blood she saw. Looking down at her nightgown and not seeing any blood, she slowly pulls her gown above her hips with tears streaming down her face as the lower part of her panties come into view.

The pain and shame begin to fill her heart as she uncovers her lower abdomen; and there it is, like graffiti on an abandoned building wall, engraved just above her hairline, "HARRIS."

She quickly covers her mouth to keep from crying aloud, and even with that, she can still hear her cry from her vocal cords echoing in the bathroom.

Visions of how good they were in the beginning, how much she really loved him, and how much he claimed to love her, are still fresh in her mind. Oddly enough, after all these years, she still tries to find the strength to forgive him. It was the only way she thought she would be able to go on with her life and not be haunted by their past.

Living alone was something she never thought about, but she knew she had to get away before he killed her. She, every now and then, would still believe that he did honestly love her, but he was too insecure about expressing it properly. Still, he had a problem and refused to accept it. She explained to him that she did not want anyone else and that he was the only one for her, but he had to make her understand as well as see, that she belonged to him and no one else.

She looks down at herself again, and she runs her fingers across the engraving, still crying...still hurting, she leans against the wall and slides down to the floor, holding her head in her hands.

"Why?" she thinks to herself. "If I ever get the chance to make him pay for what he's done to me, I promise he will regret it for the rest of his life."

No longer crying tears of sorrow, pain or betrayal these are tears of survival, anger, and vengeance that has built up over the years, of him making her inferior to him, the humiliation he caused from those unspeakable things he has done to her.

"That bastard will definitely pay if he ever tries to cross my path again." She promises and stands to splash more water on her face. She opens the medicine cabinet and reaches for a bottle of aspirin. She often suffers from migraines throughout the day, but they are unbearable after the nightmares and, she has no idea how to make them stop. She stares at herself in the mirror and remembers how beautiful he would say she was and how she really believed it and believed him.

"Oh god, how could I have been so stupid?!?" she thinks silently. She feels disgusting and filthy; she cannot bear facing herself in the mirror anymore. She doesn't even want to be a part of her own body.

"You are the most beautiful wife a man could have," his voice echoes in her mind. She forcefully presses her hands against her ears to drown out his voice. She cries so hard that it is almost impossible to suppress the sounds that are trying to escape her. His presence seems to surround her, as if his hands and breathe all over her body.

"God, please make it stop...please, God!" She begs in silence, crying as she nearly rips her nightgown off to wash away the filth of her stupidity for believing his lies of how much he adored her. She quickly gets in the shower and begins scrubbing every inch of her body with a loofa and scalding hot water. Despite the scorching heat of the water brutalizing her skin, she can only feel the humiliation of her past upon her body like a gummy stickiness that won't go away. She scrubs until the waters run cool, wraps herself in a towel and leaves the bathroom, avoiding her reflection.

While Brooklyn still lay sleeping, Chelsea steps to her vanity remove the bottom interior fabric of the drawer and grab the key to the upstairs door, where she goes up locking the door behind her.

***

It is six in the morning, and Chelsea is sitting at the kitchen table sipping on a hot cup of coffee, watching the sun greet the blackish – blue sky. When Brooklyn walks drowsily into the kitchen, stretching and yawning.

"Good morning." She greets. "Were you able to get back to sleep last night?"

"Morning, ...did, you sleep well last night?" Chelsea asks, avoiding the question.

"It was awkward, but then again, I did sleep at the bottom of your bed with your feet in my stomach...other than that, I slept fine."

"Do you want any coffee, Brook?"

"Oh yeah, that would definitely hit the spot."

"So, what are your plans for today?" Chelsea asks.

"Well, I really need to get home and water my plants and do some laundry. I'll probably loaf around after that, What about you?"

"I'll probably just hang around the house, rake the leaves and clean the gazebo." She replies, restlessly.

"By the way, Chels; what in the hell were you dreaming about last night? You were screaming and kicking like you were being attacked."

"Oh, girl...that was nothing but a bad

dream."

"What was it about?"

"I don't remember; I just got up and splashed my face with some cold water and went back to sleep."

"You know Chels; I read somewhere once that your dreams are things that will happen in the future, like a premonition. But the only thing about them is that no one knows when they will occur."

"Well, I'm sure that dream won't happen again."

"What do you mean, 'Again'? I thought you said you didn't remember it."

"Look, what's the big deal anyway; it was just a dumb dream, Brook! I don't believe in that type of crap anyway." She snaps.

"I'm sorry. I didn't mean anything by it." She replies sarcastically as she stands at the kitchen sink, washing her dish.

Although Chelsea is somewhat grateful that Brooklyn would be leaving soon, now that she has pushed her buttons, she feels slightly guilty for snapping at her; but there are things she needs to take care of upstairs and just doesn't want Brooklyn around when she goes to tend to them.

An hour or so later, Brooklyn walks out of the guest room with her overnight bag and heads for the front door while Chelsea sits swinging on the porch swing.

"Brook, what's wrong? Why are you leaving now?"

"You know Chels...sometimes you act like Harris still has control over your life as if you and he are still living together. But I want you to know that I'm not angry with you and I understand that you may have bad moods every now and then because of all the crap he put you through. I just hope you will not turn away everyone who tries to help you or get close to you. I love you as I love my own sister and you may not feel like you need any help, but if you are still having bad dreams about the things your insane husband did to you; I would suggest seeing a doctor about that entire trauma. It would be a lot better than dealing with it all alone." She says before giving her a hug. "I'll call you later."

Chelsea watches her pull off down the street until she can no longer see the tail end of her car anymore. She swiftly gets up and rushes through the house to retrieve the key to her secret place in the house. Placing the key in her robe pocket, she goes into the kitchen and prepares a bowl of tomato soup and ham sandwich. She very meticulously places everything on a platter with a tall glass of coke.

As she passes through the dining room, she makes a stop at the bar, pours a glass of Cognac, and proceeds to unlock the door to the upstairs. Once on the other side of the door, she sets the platter down on a small corner table made out from the wall, perhaps its intended use was to place flowers or plants; she uses it as she sees fit, and locks the door behind her.

Ascending the stairs, her office comes into view beyond the rows of the banister. There is a full bathroom at the very top of the stairs with a large window at the landing with the view of the backyard. There are two rooms beside each other, one of which has a few deadbolt locks on the outside as if to keep anything from getting out.

She sets the platter on a coffee table and taking a seat in a tall winged back chair with a deep sigh and closes her eyes for only a moment. Without moving her head in the direction of the bolted door, she slowly opens her eyes and stares at the door out of the corner of her eyes. She then looks at her computer desk, gets up and retrieve keys from the drawer, unlocks the bolted door and enters the room, locking it behind her.

The only sound that escapes the room is music by Enigma "I love you; I'll kill you," and even that can barely be heard for anyone's enjoyment outside of that room.

The telephone on her desk rings a few times before she comes out to answer it.

"Hello"

"Hey, babe. What are you doing?" Ron greets eagerly.

"Only thinking of you. Can I put you on hold for one second?"

"Sure."

She reenters the room only to turn off the music and locks the door behind her to reconnect with Ron. For only a moment, she hears a futile clinking sound in the room beside her, and for only a moment, her expression changes, and then she refocuses on Ron.

EVIL LURKS

It's Wednesday evening, the night Chelsea has been looking forward to all week. Finally, she and Ron were able to find time between their busy schedules to get together for a date. With her working from home, it is not every day they get to see each other, and if it were not for phone calls they would barely connect, but Ronald has intentions on changing their relationship.

As she prepares for her date, primping in the mirror and making sure her makeup is perfect, she cannot help reflecting on the hurt from her past. She distracts herself by examining her figure and smoothing her hands down the side of her waist and hips, trying, to convince herself that her beauty is true and not to be abused the way it has been by Harris, but the thought only frustrates her and reminds her of his sadistic appreciation for the beauty he often praised. She looks at her watch and recalls Ronald saying he would arrive at seven-thirty to pick her up. Having at least another fifteen minutes to kill, she goes into the dining room, behind the bar, pours a glass of white wine and takes a seat behind the bar.
With her elbows resting on the bar, sipping her wine, she recalls a pleasant memory of her

marriage back in the mid-eighties. There was a reserved spot for a family reunion in Detroit on Belle Isle, facing Canada. As if it was the very day, she remembers clearly, from the scent of the breezes off the waters to the vibrant colors of the trees, grass, and flowers; It's one of the few pleasant memories she has of him. For the first time and what made it even more becoming, was the fact that her whole family loved him as if he had been a part of the family for years.

Lying on a blanket under an old willow tree, Harris and Chelsea watch the rest of the family mingling, eating and children running around playing games as they talked about what their life would be like in the next five years.

"You'll be pregnant with our fifth child while the other four boys are playing football in the backyard of the white picket fence, I know you want." He teases.

"Yeah right, and after that fifth child, I'll be out of the house and working while you're at home with them, cooking, cleaning and going to PTA meeting every two weeks." She replied jokingly.

"Oh, you got jokes." He eases his arm around her waist and begins to tickle her.
Unbeknownst to them, they have created an audience to their outburst of laughter and playful activity, that drew in a group of first or

second cousin children joining in on their moment, with one child landing on Harris' back with their arms wrapped around his neck and another clinging to Chelsea's leg.

"Chels..." Harris called out playfully. "Help me... the aliens have captured me!"

"I'm trying but, something has a hold of my leg, and I can't get away! What are we going to do?" she teased as they took hold of the children. A flash of headlights approaching her driveway brings her back to the present, where she notices a tear forming on the edge of her eyes and quickly wipes it away on her way to look out of the window to make sure it is Ronald. The Jaguar emblem confirms it is him.

She takes another sip of her wine before going to the door, just to give him time to at least ring the bell or knock. As she passes her bedroom door, she looks over herself in the mirror a short distance from the doorframe of the bedroom. The doorbell rings and raises a girlish excitement within her. Almost giddy, she rushes to the door and opens it.

"Hey, Love!" Ronald greets with a dozen red roses and a kiss. "You look gorgeous."

"Thank you. You clean up pretty nicely yourself." She replies. "Come in. I'll be only a second. I need to get my coat."

As she walks away, Ronald can't believe his eyes and how much more beautiful she is when she puts effort into it. He has never seen her with anything other than long skirt and dark tights with her hair pinned loosely to the top of her head, but tonight, she has her hair in a nice French roll with neat tassels of hair in the back and on the sides, shining like a black mink. Her little black dress snugs her body, accentuating her every curve. Impressed and proud, Ronald can't wait to get the evening going.

***

As they enter Ruth's Chris restaurant, the host greets them asking their name while a young man takes their coats and hands them a coat check ticket.

"Thorn, the party of two," Ronald replies.

"Your table is ready, just follow the waitress."

"Thank you." Chelsea and Ronald respond simultaneously.

Feeling Ronald's hand on the small of her back as they are led to their table, gives her a special feeling that she never thought she would feel again; a sense of respect and appreciation for whom she is.

"Here you are." The server offers them a booth off in the corner as Ronald requested when he made the reservations. "Here is the wine list, sir."

"Thank you, but we'll have the Pinot Noir, Belle Glos."

"Very good sir. I'll be right back."

Chelsea can't resist staring at Ronald and thinking to herself, *"how could I've been so stupid all those years. I should have left Harris long before I decided to..."*

Turning his attention back to Chelsea, he can see that she is in a daze and has drifted off so far that she was not aware that he was now speaking to her.

"Chelsea..." he calls with a soft touch to the back of her hand.

"Hmm...yes? I'm sorry, I didn't mean-" she begins with an embarrassing look upon her face.

"No apologies are necessary." He interrupts. "Evidently, you have something on your mind. I just hope it has something to do with me."

"As a matter of fact, it was about you and needless to say, they were nice thoughts."

"I'm flattered. Would you mind telling me more about your thoughts of me?"

"Of course, I mind. They're my private thoughts and for me to know and you to find out." She teases.

"Well, I think I'd much rather be surprised then. There's a lot about you that surprises me. It seems the more I learn about you, the more I-I...want to be surprised."

"Really? And what may I ask, is so

surprising about, me?"

"Well, let's see...when I first saw you at the office, I thought you were so beautiful that I thought you were probably conceited and had a lot of men at your heels. Then to my surprise, I was wrong; and tonight...when you answered the door, you looked more beautiful than the first time I laid eyes on you. I was even hoping that you couldn't tell how nervous I was."

Feeling nauseous for every time he says the word 'beautiful,' she wants to tell him so badly, "*please stop saying that word*" but instead, she attempts to change the subject.

"So enough about me, tell me something about you that I don't already know." She says.

"Like what? You already know the significant things to keep us moving forward."

"Are you ready to order sir?" Interrupts the server.

"Yes. What would you like Love?"

"I'll have the filet mignon, potatoes au gratin, and asparagus." Chelsea answers.

"I'll have the same."

"Very good sir." The waiter says before walking away.

"I'd like to know if you've ever been married before?" Chelsea asks.

"Let's talk about something more pleasant." He replies.

His suggestion is sincere and stern as he picks

up his wine and takes a couple of gulps that nearly empties his glass.

"Ron, did I say something wrong?"

"No love."

"Well, what's wrong?"

"I know that we've been seeing each other for about a year now, and I enjoy being with you so much that I don't want to waste valuable time going into unpleasant discussions. Can you understand that?"

"Sure; but now it seems like you have something to hide and I feel that if we plan to move forward, these are some of the things we don't need coming out later in the relationship where one of us may get hurt."

"I respect that, but some things are difficult for me to talk about, and I hope that you'll be a little patient with me."

Even though her curiosity is at its peak, she was not going to press the issue. After all, there are things that she does not plan to talk about either...not even to Brooklyn as long as she still has breath in her body.

"Alright, I'm sorry if I stirred up any unpleasant memories." She apologizes.

"No need for apologies, babe. There will come a day when I am able to stop feeling horrible about my past, and I'm able to put it all behind me, then I'll be able to, talk about it without prejudice, you'll be the first to hear about it."

The words, *'put it all behind me'* repeats in her mind as she gazes out of the window, watching the first few drops of rainfall and the lightning flash across the sky.

Thoughts of the things that happened one night when Harris came home from the bar began to play in her mind. She leaned her shoulder and tilted her head against the window; the abuse was so deep inside her, she often wondered if she would ever be able to put it all behind her.

"Chelsea, why are you crying babe? I swear it's nothing that bad..."

"Please excuse me. I need to go to the ladies' room." She stands with her purse in hand.

"Are you alright?" he asks as he stands courteously for her. "Do you want to leave?"

"Please, Ron, I'm fine. Just give me a minute to freshen up." She asks, obviously trying to cover up the cracking in her voice.

"I'm going to take care of the check, and we can leave when you get back, okay?"

"No. Really, I'm going to be just fine. Let's keep it a pleasant evening. I swear I'll be better when I come back from the ladies' room."

***

Chelsea returns with her makeup fresh and a pleasant smile on her face. Ronald stands upon her entering and taking her hand as she sits.

"I'm sorry about that." She apologizes.

"No. Let me apologize. I understand and respect that these are things we need to talk about and I'm sorry if I hurt you by not wanting to talk about it, and I will tell you anything you want to know."

"It's not that, Ron. It's me, and someday I will be able to be more open with you as well. It's just that some things from my past run so deep, it's hard to talk about, but they sit right on the surface of my current life. So, I completely understand where you're coming from."

"You surprise me once more."

"Oh?"

"We apparently have baggage we need to work through. Which makes us even more compatible." He says with a wink and a smile as the server approaches with their meal.

"Mmm, this looks wonderful!" Chelsea comments pleasantly. "I have an idea…"

"Oh?"

"Tell me what you were like as a child."

"Ahh, that is a good idea. What do you want to know? If I was a hard-headed little boy? Defiant, or a bully?"

"Anything. How about the most memorable part of your childhood?"

"Ok. Well, for starters, I was just like any little boy that loved riding his big wheel and making believe I was my favorite superhero. One incident I recall vividly, was when I was about eight years old, and a friend of mine, and I competing on who could jump the furthest from the porch of an abandoned house."

"Who won?"

"I never found out. When it was my turn to jump, I landed on a broken coke cola bottle that went through my knee, my sister ran home, told my grandmother, and I was rushed to the hospital."

"Oh my god! Leave it to boys to get themselves hurt like that."

"Ok; what about you? What do you remember the most about your childhood?"

"I don't recall getting injured like that but...I did do something that I'll never forget, and it's a little embarrassing so... don't laugh."

"I won't." He smiles. "What did you do?"

"I think I was around the same age as you, maybe a little younger when I found a small black spray can. I went to my mother while she was in the bathroom, putting on makeup and asked her what it was. The only thing she told me was to put it back and leave it alone."

"Oh lord...honey this doesn't sound too good. Please tell me you put it back." Ron comments, taking a bite of his steak and a sip of wine.

"Not before taking it to the back of the house in the kitchen and sprayed it like it was air freshener and continuing through the dining

room. By the time I got to the dining room, my dog and bird were coughing and hacking. I took them out to the porch; it was the dead of winter in Detroit. Before I knew it, my mother was at my heels coughing, choking and yelling at me with mascara and eyeliner running down her face, asking me what I had done."
Before Chelsea could finish the story, Ronald was already laughing and trying not to choke on his food.

"I told you not to laugh." She reminds him with a grin.

"You didn't ask me to promise, so you can't hold it against me, but I can only imagine your mothers face as she approached you. That is hilarious!" He continues to laugh. "That is the best damn story I've ever heard. You can't make that stuff up."

"I didn't...that was the worst beating I got that day. How was I supposed to know that it was mace? She only told me to leave it alone; she didn't tell me what it was or what it was for."

"That's a great story Love. You have my stomach hurting." He continues laughing.

"You have a great laugh." She says admirably.

"Thank you. I enjoy your company and would like to be able to spend more time with you, but it seems that your best friend keeps that from happening."

"Oh yes; Brooklyn. You two will meet. I will tell you this much about her from my eyes. She is like a sister to me, but there are times when she is a little overprotective, and I feel like she is my mother. I know she means well, but she tends to be a bit bold at times, and it seems to come at the not so appropriate time. Don't get me wrong, I love her to death. She's been there for me through thick and thin, and I never want to lose that."

"You shouldn't have to, not even for me. I respect the bond you and she have, but I feel like I can't get any closer to you because of he, and that seems to be by your choice, not hers. Is there a reason you put her before us?"

"I just know she wouldn't have a problem getting in your face and letting you know that she will watch you very closely to make sure you don't hurt me."

"Hmm, ok; I like her already. There is nothing that I would do to intentionally hurt you." He replies, sincerely.

"I appreciate that, and I will make a point to let the two of you meet."

***

The car ride back to Chelsea's house is very romantic and lovable with hand holding, cuddles, and nearly no conversation. The roads were getting worse as the rain began to fall harder with thunder and lightning vibrating the earth.

"I didn't realize it was going to get this bad." Ron comments.

"I heard something on the radio, but, you're right, they didn't say anything about thunderstorms."

"Are you going to be alright alone, or would you like some company?"

"I'll be fine; you should probably get right home before it gets any worst out here."

"I guess you're right, I left a few windows open to let in some fresh air. My curtains are probably soaked."

Once they return to her house, Ron shields Chelsea with his jacket from the rain as he walks her to her door. She turns on the lamp beside the sofa as soon as she enters the living room. He helps her with her coat and lays it across the back of the dining chair.

"I hope I didn't sound too aggressive when you asked me about being married?"

"Oh, no...why, would you think that?"

"Well, you starting crying, and I want to apologize coming off harshly when you asked."

"You were not aggressive at all and don't think that you did or said anything to upset me, alright?"

"Okay, ...but, what happened, why were you crying?"

"Well, it's just like you said earlier, 'some things are difficult to talk about,' and when I'm able to put them behind me, they won't trouble me anymore."

"I respect that." He replies, taking her into his arms. "But I want you to know that no matter what, you can call on me for anything. Even if it's just for a shoulder to cry on. If there is anything, I can do to make you feel better or to help, I will die trying, and you can count on that. You mean more to me than you probably think."

Upon those words, she squeezes him tightly, silently thinking; "*I wish I could believe that. I feel so safe right now, please don't let me go. Would you understand the reasons why I stayed with Harris for so long, or would you judge me for my stupidity?*"

"Now you get comfortable, and I'll make you a hot cup of tea." He says,

"Thank you, Ron, but you don't have to do that. It's late, and I know you're probably tired."

"Yes, but I don't want you to feel like I'm some non-caring asshole."

"You're sweet, and I know you are. Your efforts alone speak volumes, and until you do or say otherwise, I will let you know. I am fine, really. I'm just going to soak in the tub then curl up with a book and hot tea. I'll be alright. I promise." She says with a smile.

"Alright, if you insist." He replies, walking towards the door to leave. "But, if you need anything, give me a call. No matter what time it is, okay?"

"Okay, Ron."

She walks him to the door and gives him a kiss goodnight. He tells her he loves her and that he means every word he said.

Locking the door behind him, she listens for his engine start, and drive away.

She goes into the kitchen to turn the kettle off and makes a cup of tea. She can hear the rain hitting the window as she reaches into the cabinet for a cup in hand, she pulls back the curtain to see how bad it is raining. While peering out of the window, lightning flashes across the sky, providing momentary light in the yard. Within that few seconds of light, there is a figure of someone sitting in the gazebo, and at that moment, her heart starts to pound with fear of who could be in her yard.

She convinces herself that it is probably the shadow of the rose bush, but when the lightning flashes again, the figure is gone, and the yard is black as a hole. Still looking out the window, waiting for another flash of lightning to confirm what she has or has not seen. Startled by the telephone ringing the cup falls from her hand and breaks into the sink. Again, the phone rings but, the fear inside her keeps her from moving...another ring and she slowly walks over and puts her hand on the receiver.

"Hel-hello?" She answers, trying to conceal the panic in her voice. She can only hear static in return.

"The storm must be affecting the phone lines." She thinks out loud, but, as she pulls the phone away to hang up, she hears a voice.

"Hello?" she calls out, putting the phone back to her ear.

"Are you missing me?" the caller says, with too much static to be understood.

"Who is this?" She demands. The static is louder, and the voice is breaking up.

"Didn't - I - tell - not - me? I - you - find you didn't -believe me." The voice continues as the static grows louder, and the voice fades. Frightened, she hangs up the phone and automatically, dials 911, and as the receiving end rings, she hears noises in the yard that sounds like someone throwing rocks in the well. At the same time, she wonders who was on the other end of the call.

"Well, the police should be here soon enough, and once they go around the house, I'll feel better." She thinks to herself, looking up at the clock.

Time seems to tick away slowly as she waits for the police to arrive. She grows more and more concerned about the phone call.

There is a clatter at the dining room window, but she is too afraid to pull back the curtain to look out.

"Whoever is out there, I'll have you know that the police are on their way, so I suggest you leave." She yells out loud.

The storm seems to have passed even though the thunder continues with trails of lightning following it. There's a banging on the front door that startles her, once again.

"Who is it!?"

"Police, we received a call from this residence."

"Oh, thank god!" She runs to the door and throws it open. "While I was in the kitchen, I swear I saw someone in the gazebo in my backyard, and then I got a phone call that I couldn't make out what was being said but, that could be because of the storm, and then I heard a clattering noise at the window there in the dining room." She informs in a panic.

"Calm down, Miss. Let's take this slow." the officer says, pulling out a small note pad and pencil. "What is your name?"

"I'm Chelsea, Webber."

"Ok. I'm Officer Taylor, and my partner officer Williams is checking out the perimeter of your house now."

"That's good, thank you."

"Now about the person, you saw in the

yard; did you see the person's face at all?"

"No, it's too dark. The only thing I could make out was the silhouette of a person."

"Did they appear to have a weapon or something in their hand?"

"Well, I can't say for sure, but it looked as if they may have had a stick or a cane."

"Did they make an attempt to enter your home at all?"

"Well, I didn't hear anything until I was on the telephone."

"Was this clatter like a branch or bush hitting the window, or did it sound like someone was trying to come in?"

"I don't know!" She replies a bit frustrated. "I guess like someone was trying to pull the window open. Officer Taylor, shouldn't you go out there and see if they're still there hiding or something?"

"Miss Webber, I told you that my, partner is already out there taking care of that."

Chelsea goes to the kitchen window, pulls back the curtain, and looks into the yard, where she can see an officer with his flashlight walking towards her back door. She walks over to let the officer in, and as he steps inside, he has a peculiar look upon his face.

"Good evening, ma'am. I'm officer Williams. Is my partner inside the house?"

"Yes, he's there in the-"

"Here I am Williams." Officer Taylor calls from the dining room.

"Excuse me, ma'am." He says as he walks towards Officer Taylor and begins to whisper his findings of the perimeter.

"Hey, what's going on?" Chelsea interrupts.

"Miss Webber, we have received quite a few calls from this area reporting a prowler, and the good thing is that there haven't been any reports of burglary or home invasion. But, since you're the third person that has reported this, we'll have an unmarked police officer on your street as well as the block in front and behind you."

"Wait a minute...is this person dangerous? Did he escape from prison or something and how long have you been getting complaints about this?"

"First of all, we have no reports of anyone escaping jail or prison for all we know this could be someone looking for shelter from the storm. But for your safety, lock up your house and if you see anyone looking suspicious, don't hesitate to call us again. By the way, if you're not using that old well back there, you should have it sealed up to prevent any accidents. You never know when an unsupervised child may come into your yard and let curiosity get the best of them and fall in."

"Thank you. I'll look into that right away."

"Have a good evening, ma'am, and here's my card." Officer Taylor says as he steps onto the porch to leave.
Still a bit uneasy, Chelsea picks up the phone and calls Brooklyn to let her know what is going on and to warn her to lock up her place.

"We're sorry, the number you have dialed is being checked for trouble. Please try your call later."

"Damn! That storm must have hit hard in Alexandria. I hope it hasn't caused too much damage. I'll try her again tomorrow." She thinks aloud.

WTF HAPPENED

It is seven-thirty and the morning news is on the television in the living room, while Chelsea is in the kitchen making her breakfast before her nine-thirty client meeting.

"In Alexandria, a woman was found severely beaten..." the news anchor reports.

"Oh my god!" Chelsea says, running into the living room to catch the story.

"...unconscious at this apartment building last night. Apparently, the woman was returning home from the grocery store when a man, who witnesses say, was wearing blue jeans, and a long black coat attacked her. The suspect is said to be, in his mid to early thirties, six feet tall and weighing one 200 pounds. The police have not ruled out foul play. The woman is now in hospital care listed in critical condition. The name of the victim has not yet been released until family members are notified. The police are advising not to confront this person but to call the one eight hundred on your screen or your local police department. When we return, we will give you the latest on the Beltway traffic and weather.

Chelsea sits almost paralyzed from the site of Brooklyn's apartment building on the news practically surrounded with yellow strips of the 'Police do not cross' tape. Not wanting to think the worst, yet having that prickly feeling in her stomach, she immediately picks up the phone and dials Brooklyn, only to hear the same recording she heard last night. Still hoping for the better, she calls the hospital where Brooklyn works as a nurse in the psychiatric ward.

"Hello, may I speak with nurse Brooklyn Brown?" she, asks nervously.

"Nurse Brown...?"

"Yes. This I'm her friend Chelsea Webber. Is she working today?"

"Hi, Chelsea, this is Amber."

"Hey, Amber. Is Brook working today?"

"Oh, Chels! She was admitted late last night."

Fear and guilt build in the pit of her stomach as the voice of their friend goes faint to her ear.

"Is she alright? Why was she admitted?"

"Apparently she was assaulted pretty bad last night. But, she's in good hands now."

Chelsea's mind begins to race. Frantically she looks all around for her keys only to find them right beside the telephone.

***

She arrives at Mount Vernon Hospital in a panic, nearly hitting a parked car as she pulls into a parking space. She manages to hit a car with her door as she jumps out and runs through the parking lot to the hospital waiting room.

"I need to see Brooklyn Brown, please!"

"I'm sorry ma'am, but no one is authorized to visit her except family unless you're on the visiting list. Is your name on the list?"

"I don't know..." Chelsea replies nearly ready to cry.

"What's your name, and I'll check?"

"Chelsea, Webber."

Just as the nurse begins to thumb through the file, another nurse and mutual friend of Chelsea and Brooklyn's comes from around the corner.

"Chelsea?"

"Oh, Karen, how is Brook? Will she be all right? Can I see her?"

"Well, she was unconscious when they brought her in last night, but she is conscious now. She had some bleeding on her brain, and the doctors performed surgery to fix that from further damage."

"Can I see her, Karen?"

"Well, I don't want to go against the family's request if your name isn't on the list, they provided us. Plus, the doctor is in there with her now." Karen replies, apologetically.

"Would you mind checking?"

Karen picks up the file that the other nurse set aside and begins looking through it as Chelsea stands with her arms resting on the counter, tapping her fingernails along the top of the counter in an irritating manner.

"You're on the list Chels. But the doctor is in with her right now. You may go in when you see her comes out."

"Thank you so much!" She replies, following Karen towards the visitor's waiting room. While waiting for the doctor to leave, Chelsea sits trying to calm herself to prepare her mind for whatever condition Brooklyn may be in as well as, wondering who would have done this to her.

"Chels, you can go in and see her now."

"Thanks again, Karen."

Slowly and quietly, Chelsea enters the room. As she steps closer to the bed, Brooklyn's face comes into view. Chelsea is stunned that she can hardly recognize her best friend. Tears begin to fill her eyes as she becomes angry with herself for not being there for her, and most of all, how she treated her the day before. She's heartbroken to see Brooklyn's face swollen and disfigured with bruises of green and purple all around her eyes, lips, and cheeks. She pulls a chair closer to the bed and with a trembling hand; she takes Brooklyn's hand in hers. Brooklyn slowly opens her eyes as she gives as much of a warm smile as possible, then her expression turns to pure terror. She begins to grab Chelsea's hand tighter as the terror in her eyes grow more intense and concerning.

"Brook, you're going to be alright honey. I promise you'll be just fine."

"Here...um...um!"

"Brook, take your time, honey. What are you trying to say?"

"Hurt...um...hurt!" she tries to speak more strongly.

"Shhh, save your energy. Let me do the talking, okay? Don't get yourself all worked up, you should try to relax!"

"He...um...hurt...um!" She expresses even louder, causing the nurses to come into the room and escort Chelsea out to the waiting room.

"What's going on? She's trying to tell me something! Why can't I stay?"

"I'm sorry, but the doctor will have to speak to you. I thought you knew since you were on the list." Karen says.

"Know what? What is it that I should know, please, Karen, tell me?"

"I can't. I'll call Dr. Deloach and have her talk to you, ok? Just sit here and calm down." Chelsea sits on the edge of her seat with her elbows on her knees, face in her hands, crying profusely, trying to absorb the appearance of her best friend. Frustration builds from feeling helpless and useless to Brooklyn.

"Mrs. Webber?"

"It's Ms."

"My apologies. I'm Dr. Deloach. I'm the neurologist on the team of doctors caring for Miss Brown."

"Oh, thank god! Please tell me what's going on. Why can't I finish my visit? She's trying to tell me something important."

"I understand your frustration, but I need you to remain as calm as possible. Miss Brown has to remain calm because otherwise, her head injuries may cause her a stroke."

"Ok, I'm sorry. It's just that I can tell by the look in her eyes that she's trying to tell me something important."

"Well, we were told by the family that you and Miss Brown are as close as sisters? Therefore, I assume that the family informed you of her condition, but it did not dawn on me that they might not have been able to reach you due to last night's storm. Even I was without power."

"Yes...I understand. With all of this, my mind is only focused on Brook."

"I absolutely understand."

"Please tell me what I need to know about her condition."

"Well, Miss Brown obtained extensive damage to the left front side of her brain, causing her to have a speech impairment."

"How severe is the impairment? I mean, she was just trying to tell me something."

"What she has is expressive aphasia, which means that she knows what she wants to say, yet has difficulty communicating it to others."

"How severe is it for her?"

"She is unable to understand spoken and written words into something that we can understand so, even if you try to communicate with her in writing she will not understand what you write or how to write a response. She struggles with knowing the right words to say."

"Doctor, she had a terrifying look in her eyes when she saw me. Does she even recognize me? Is this treatable?" Chelsea asks, wiping away tears.

Before the doctor can answer, she is paged, both by beeper and over the hospital intercom. "STAT," although faint to Chelsea's ears, it is loud and clear to Dr. Deloach.

"Ms. Webber, my apologies. I'm being called to the emergency room. I would tell you to wait, but I have no idea how long I'll be."

"I understand. Thank you so much, doctor." She says as the doctor runs off down the hallway.

"Chels, you can go back in now if you want to. I've given Brook a small dose of a sedative to keep her from getting too excited."

"Thanks again, Karen, I really do appreciate

it."

"It's ok. Just try not to get her too excited; ok?"

"Okay. I won't be too long." She says as she makes her way back into Brooklyn's room.

As Brooklyn comes into view beyond the pulled curtain, Chelsea tries to wipe away all signs of distress from her face, including wiping away tears and trying to smile warmly.

"Brook, I'm sorry about what happened, and I want you to know that I'm sorry for starting that fight with you too. I miss you."

"Um...um...hurt."

"I know sweetie, and if I find out who did this to you, I swear I'll kill them."

"Um...hurt...mmm...mmm." She says rather drowsily.

"I'm going to let you get your rest, and I'll come by and see you tomorrow." She says, rubbing the back of Brook's hand as she stands to leave. "I love you, girl."

As she leaves the hospital, she stops by the nurse's station to see Karen and asks her to keep her abreast of Brooklyn's condition.

*

Sitting in her car, she rests her head on the steering wheel with her eyes closed trying to remove the image of Brooklyn's face and head and wondering who and why anyone would want to hurt her. Wondering if this is just some random incident or was it, someone she knew, she wipes the tears from her eyes and puts the key in the ignition.

Hypnotized by the condition of her friend, she drives home on familiar roads practically going through stop signs and red traffic lights and more often than not, she'd sit through a green light until someone blows their horn, snapping her out of her haze.

By the time she gets home, she sees her nine-thirty appointment is sitting on her porch swing waiting patiently for her return.

"Oh, shit! I totally forgot about them." She sighs, with a smile to them as she pulls into the driveway and waves.

"I'm so sorry. I hope you weren't waiting too long."

"We're actually late and really just got here, so I hope we can still fit the timeslot." The client says.

"Well, to be honest, there has been a tragic event in the family, and I'm not sure if I'll be attentive enough to your needs. But if you come inside, I will give you my team member's contact, and you can work with her. I am so sorry. She and I work very closely on your designs, and she will assist you until I can get this family matter resolved. I hope you understand."

"I'm sorry that things are bad, and if you

want, I can wait until you get things worked out."

"I appreciate that but, it isn't fair for me to leave you hanging and I have no idea how long this situation is going to take before…I'm sorry, I just can't." She says, trying to hold back tears. "Here is my partner's card. She has your portfolio in hand, and I promise you, you will not be disappointed."

"Alright. I'll give her a call. Is she willing to come from DC to me?"

"Yes. Again, my apologies but this can't be helped." Chelsea says, escorting the client to the door.

"I hope things turn out for the better for your family member."

"Thank you; so, do I."

**

Around eleven-thirty and a couple of hours of crying and coming to grips with the reality of the events, Chelsea begins to pull herself together a bit. By late afternoon, she is out back raking leaves in an effort of clearing her mind. The afternoon seems eerily quiet as the rake against the leaves and grass seems to echo in the air. She pauses for a moment and realizes that she is the one breaking the silence. She drops the rake on the pile of leaves and takes a seat in the gazebo. While sitting there staring at the leaves on the ground blowing in the wind, she remembers a time when she and Brooklyn were just teenagers and had a sleepover. They snuck out of the house to go to a party. The memory puts half a smile on her face.

Her fondest memory was a time when they were eight years old, and school was out for the summer. It was their favorite thing to stay up late and be able to play outside at night, pretending to be spies. They would hide behind bushes whispering to each other to keep from being heard.

"*Look, Brook! Those teenagers are getting it on over there at the playground on the slide!*"

"*No way!*" Brook whispers as she gets a closer look peering through the bushes.

"*Yes, way; and they're naked!*" Chelsea whispers and grins.

"*Ewe! I'm never getting on that slide again! That's nasty!*"

Chelsea chuckles out loud as she brings herself back to the present and realizes how much the two of them have actually known each other and how Brooklyn was always stronger than her and always had her back. She never showed a sign of weakness to a man and, she never let a man come between their friendship. She always encouraged Chelsea to be more authoritative with her life and not let people walk all over her, but try as she might, she was never that sure of herself.

"I have to be stronger for her. I can't let her down!" She says to herself.

Mixed emotions begin to rise and infuriate her as she recalls a photographic image of Brooklyn in the hospital with bruises on her face and head; Chelsea begins to feel the toughness that Brooklyn always protected her with.

On her way back into the house, she hears the telephone ringing and runs into the house to catch the call.

"Hello."

"Hey, babe. How are you?"

"Oh, Ron! Something terrible has happened!"

"What is it? Do you need me to come over?"

"Brooklyn was attacked last night, and she's in the hospital."

"Sweetheart, why didn't you call me?"

"I'm sorry...I'm still a bit in shock."

"Babe, what happened?"

"I was watching the news this morning about an attack in Alexandria and decided to call Brook since she lives there, to see if she heard anything and it turned out to be her that was attacked!"

"Oh, my god, babe. I am so sorry. Is she going to be alright?"

"She has lost her ability to communicate; therefore, she can't tell anyone who her attacker or what they look like. This is all my fault."

"How is this, your fault?"

"I purposely argued with her so she would leave the other day, and now I can't even apologize to her for it."

"Sweetheart, that doesn't make what happened to her your fault. You're just feeling guilty that you fell out with her, and that doesn't make any of this your fault. How are you doing? Are you ok?"

"I'm ok, just a little tired. I haven't eaten all day, and I don't have an appetite."

"Well, you have to eat something to keep your strength up for when you see her again. Would you like me to bring you something?"

"Thank you, Ron, but I'm just going to lay down and try to take a nap."

"Well, you call me if you need anything; alright?"

"I will. Thank you. I'll give you a call tomorrow."

"Hey, would you like me to go with you when you go to see her again?"

"I think that would be nice. I'll let you know."

EVIL IS...

It is six-thirty in the evening, the telephone rings.
"Hello." Chelsea answers.
"Hey, beautiful, how was your day?" Harris asks.
"It was ok."
"I'm just calling to let you know that Wayne and Tony are coming by to go over this case; we go to court for it on Monday. So, set two extra places for dinner, okay?"
"Sure. Are you coming straight home, or are you going to make your usual stop at the Black Orchid?"
"I should be straight home; we really need to start working on this case."
"Alright, then. I'll see you soon."
Two hours later, there is no sign of Harris or a phone call. Chelsea keeps the food warm for as long as she can without drying it out, and with her being six months pregnant, she tires easily. She prepares individual plates, wraps them up, sets them on the stove and heads up to go to bed and goes to sleep.

**

By one-thirty in the morning, she's awakened by the sound of laughter and loud talking. She knows Harris has been drinking, and there is no telling how long they are going to be awake. She

puts her pillow over her ear and pulls the blanket up over her head to drown out the noise.
"Chelsea!" He calls from the bottom of the stairs.
"Hey, man, she's probably asleep. Let her be." One of the guys says.
"She was supposed to have dinner ready for us, Tony, and I don't see the table set. I don't know about you, but I'm hungry. Chelsea come down here!" He yells again.
She gets out of bed and goes to the top of the stairs.
"What is it, Harris?"
"Come down and fix us something to eat."
"I put the dinner on the stove for you, so when you're done, just put it in the refrigerator."
"I told you that I have to work on this case. I don't have time to go in there and fix everybody a plate. Now come on down here!"
"Harris, it's late, and I'm tired. I've made individual plates there on the stove, so just heat it up." She says before going back to bed.
Before she can get back into a comfortable position, he is already in the room nudging her shoulder telling her to heat up their food with the smell of alcohol on his breath.
"Alright Harris, but after that, I'm going back to sleep; so, don't bother me anymore after that." *She says getting out of bed and putting on a robe. After serving them their plates, Harris continues*

to make a nuisance of himself. Every time she walks away to go to bed, he asks her for something else, first salt, then napkins then a drink.

"Harris, if you need anything else you know exactly where to find it. Fella's make yourselves at home if there is anything you need. Good night."

"Wait a minute, I know you're not trying to embarrass me in front of my colleagues!" he says following to the bedroom.

"I don't know what you're talking about, Harris."

He helps her into bed, he pulls the covers up to her shoulders and without warning, he swiftly palms her neck into his hand and squeezes, pulling her face up to his while choking her. The light from the hallway becomes dim. She sees splotches of red, then green then finally everything is black.

"Don't you ever try to embarrass me again? I will kick your ass! Do you understand me? I will kill you!" He threatens, pushing her head into the pillow, before releasing his grip. She tries to catch her breath through coughs as he hands her the glass of water she has by the bed.

"Don't come near me again!" She says slapping the glass out of his hand.

"Oh, really! What do you think you're going to do to me if I do?"

"Just stay the hell away from me, Harris."

He stumbles out of the room and back downstairs to his friends where she can hear them asking if everything was alright or if they should leave to which Harris's only reply is, 'How about another beer.'

Upset and fearful, it is hard to get any sleep, especially with all the noise they were making down there. She gets up, closes the door. She lays in bed somewhat grateful that his friends are still there because she knows; he will not be bothering her for as long as they are visiting. Eventually, she falls asleep but not without thoughts of pressing charges against him and leaving him for good.

**

"Get up!"

"Harris, what is it?"

"Get your ass up!" He grabs her by the elbow, pulling her out of bed and dragging her down the stairs.

"My god Harris, it's four-thirty in the morning. What could you possibly need now?"

"I know that you're thinking about leaving me...and that's not going to happen!"

"What are you talking about? I was asleep. I wasn't thinking anything." She screams as he continues to drag her through the house and down to the basement behind the laundry room, where he keeps his weights and exercise equipment. He closes the door behind them, and *immediately Chelsea screams, as things are being knocked over and broken beyond the closed door.*

"How dare you fucking embarrass me in front of my colleagues!" he yells with the sound of his fist to her face.

Moments later he leaves the room, closing and locking the door behind him, while Chelsea hangs by her wrists by a rope battered, bruised and unconscious. He goes back up to the bedroom where he plops on the bed and falls fast asleep.

As time passes on, Chelsea regains consciousness with dull pains in her lower back and belly. She feels the need to lift the baby a bit and finds that she is tied by the wrists. She tries as hard as she can to practice her Kegel exercises but the weight of the baby putting pressure on her cervix and her being bound with her hands above her head doesn't allow much relief for her. Not knowing how long she's been hanging there she's concerned about the baby and begins to scream for help and with every yell for help her head throbs with pain from the beating Harris gave her, but she continues despite the pain, only to find her plea falls on deaf ears of those that might care.

**

The sun beams its light through the bedroom window irritating Harris's drunken slumber. He wakes up with a throbbing headache and nauseous but; he has a remedy for it. He goes into

the bathroom where he keeps a hidden stash of vodka in the linen closet and takes a couple of gulps before hopping into the shower and brushing his teeth.
Later in the afternoon, he decides to unlock the door to let Chelsea out, but he begins to worry when he sees that she has blood running down her legs and on to the floor. This is probably the first time that he showed any concern for their unborn baby. He rushes in grabbing her by the waist as he cuts her loose.

"Harris, I need to go to the hospital." She cries.

"Don't worry. I'll call the doctor to come over."

"They don't make house calls anymore. I need to go to the emergency room, please."

"No! You're going to stay right here at home." He demands as he carries her up to their bedroom.

"You can't get a doctor out here, Harris."

"Shut up! I know what to do."

"Oh my god! Please don't hurt me anymore."

"I'm not going to hurt you. You just lay here and let me get you cleaned up, and I'll have someone come take a look at the baby."

"You're not making any sense, Harris."
He rushes around the bedroom to the bathroom to clean, the blood from her before he makes his call, but she slowly loses consciousness from the

loss of blood and fatigue. He begins to panic and tries to wake her with taps to her cheeks and a cool cloth to her forehead and neck to which he gets no response. Quickly he picks up the telephone calling on a doctor that he defended years back for sexual assault on a patient under anesthesia that he ultimately had given an STD to. As he dials the number, he recalls the doctor telling him that he owed him one for getting him acquitted of the charges.

*

Thirty minutes later, the doorbell rings causing a sense of relief to Harris as he runs down the stairs, nearly losing his footing and practically in tears.

"Where is she?" The doctor asks.

"She's upstairs in the bed. I can't get her to wake up, and she hasn't stopped bleeding."

"What happened?"

"Hey, we agreed; no questions. Just do what you can for her and the baby."

"Yeah, I gotcha. But if anything goes seriously wrong with her, I wasn't here, and I didn't see her."

"Whatever you want man."

As they enter the bedroom, the doctor is taken aback by the bruises and black eye on Chelsea's face he wants to ask what happened, but he proceeds into the room and tells Harris to get a small basin with warm soapy water while he

takes her pulse and checks her temperature.
"Harris, bring a couple of towels to lay under her so I can get her cleaned up better."
"Got it."

*

After the examination, Harris is somewhat relieved to know that she isn't dying, and he will need to nurse her back to health.
"She's dehydrated, and her cervix has dilated to two centimeters. How far along is she?"
"She's six months pregnant."
"Well, you're going to have to keep her off her feet for a good while because as it stands, she could lose the baby. I gave her a little something for the pain, and she should be coming around soon. She's exhausted."
"I'll make sure she gets plenty of rest."
"Good and make sure she takes in plenty of fluids."
"I will. Thanks again for coming out."
"No problem but, no more. I'm trying to get my life right and keep my license. So, I know I owed you one, and this is it."
"I gotcha man. The next time you hear from me, it'll be legit."

**

The following day, Harris caters to her every need but, little does he know she is feeling much better than she is letting on. Day in and day out she lays comfortably plotting and planning her escape from him and ways to leave without a trace of where she's going or where she's been. Her experience has taught her that he is very good at finding her and bringing her back to him despite the protection orders against him.

Playing on his guilt and fear of thinking that he came close to killing her and their baby, benefits her more than he would ever guess. Every time he is not in her presence, she gathers clothing and toiletries in a duffle bag that she keeps hidden under the bed for an easy getaway and after a week's time of recuperating at his labor, she makes her move.

She tiptoes to the top of the stairs where she sees Harris passed out in a drunken stupor in front of the television that is blasting the eleven o'clock news at him. She runs back into the bedroom, pulls her duffle bag from under the bed, and quietly makes her way downstairs to the kitchen where she plans to leave out the back door. She grabs the tea canister where she's been stashing money for years. It has been the safest place since he hates tea. Without counting the money, she crams it into her pocket, retrieves her identification.

Thinking what she as may not be enough, she recalls his stash of recreational drugs and cash that he hides in his bowling bag. Quietly she enters the living room and to the front closet, just a couple of feet away from him. Down on her knees, she rummages through shoes and boots to get to the back of the closet where the bowling bag is. Every slight sound that she makes, she looks over her shoulder to make sure that she hasn't awakened him. She finds the money and quickly shoves it into her pocket as she runs for the back door.

*

She arrives at the Greyhound a half past midnight, and the next bus to Virginia isn't until an hour and a half. She buys her ticket and camps out in the women's restroom in case her husband wakes up and finds her gone.
Fighting sleep while sitting in a stall, she retraces her steps to make sure she's leaving no trace of where she's headed. The fear of him waiting right outside the restroom sets in the pit of her stomach. She will not feel safe until she is on the bus, and it is in motion.
The announcement, "Bus 29 to Virginia is approaching and will board in forty minutes." echoes within the building and faintly heard in the restrooms. Almost too afraid to move, she needs to look out to the lobby area for her husband or one of his flunkies. The coast is clear from what she can see but, it's too soon to risk going out there to wait in line to board. The least amount of time exposed to the public, the better her chances of not being seen and recaptured. She waits out her time up to the last five minutes

of the boarding, before leaving the restroom. She peeks her head out the door and looks around the station making sure Harris isn't there looking for her. The whole time she's waiting in line to get on the bus, she continues to be worried that her husband will be walking up on her and discreetly taking her away and back home for more abuse. She's barely breathing as she boards the bus looking for him or someone he knows. Still barely breathing, she makes herself comfortable cradling her duffle bag in her lap as if someone would steal it away from her.

The bus takes off, and is rolling at a steady pace, she finally breathes a sigh of relief with a few tears of feeling free, safe, and excited for planning a new life without pain and suffering. Surprisingly, she falls asleep after about twenty-five minutes into the ride.

***

She finds shelter with her great-grandfather in a house that he built many in 1901. He welcomes her warmly and is pleased to know that she was no longer with her husband. After she fills him in on the situation and why she is there, he takes her in and lets her know that she is at home and can stay for as long as she likes. Finally, she feels safe and among the family that loves her.

Over the next month or so Chelsea had not felt this much at peace since before she was married, she even enjoyed helping her great-grandfather out with housework and cooking and the pleasant conversations they would have every night.

It was late one night when she was awakened with massive pains to her lower back and belly. She pulls back the covers to go to the bathroom and find that she is bleeding badly, and despite the excruciating pain, she manages to keep quiet and not wake her grandfather. She walks to the door in her room that leads upstairs, and, on her hands and knees, she crawls her way up a few steps, but the pain is too intense for her to make it all the way. She feels the need to bear down and stops crawling up the stairs just to push the baby down. Quietly as possible, she groans and moans as she pushes the baby down until she feels something protruding between her legs. She reaches down and feels a tiny foot.

"Oh my God...dear God, please don't let this be this way. I just know he is waiting for me to sign into any hospital to have my baby so he can take us back to him. Please don't let it be this way! I can't live another day with that man...with or without my child! Please have mercy!" She begs audibly as the pain intensifies. Pulling herself up the steps a little further, she makes it to the landing and crawls into a room on the left side of the steps, closing the door behind her.

Two hours later, she'd given birth to a

stillborn baby girl that she names Shyer. After cleaning the baby off, exhausted and distraught, she cries herself to sleep embracing her baby close to her heart. Of all the things that Harris has put her through, not one of them has torn her apart as much as this. The thought of her baby being sacrificed for his asinine sadistic behavior just makes her hate him more than she ever thought she was capable of hating.

A month later her great-grandfather dies, leaving her everything he had. Before he died, he advised her to change her last name to somewhat make her even harder to find.

***

As time passes on, she grows lonely for her friends and family and despite what her great-grandfather told her, she calls her best friend Brooklyn, swearing her to secrecy, she tells her where she is, and it's not long after, that Brooklyn moves to Virginia landing a job at the INOVA hospital in Alexandria.

When Brooklyn arrives in town, she immediately begins telling Chelsea how much Harris was breathing down her neck about where she was moving to and why.

"You didn't tell him, did you?" Chelsea panics.

"Of course not! He would ask me every day whether I knew where you were or not. I just told him that my job moved me because of a promotion. Then he called himself threating me, by telling me if he finds out that I knew where you were all along, and didn't tell him, he was going to kill me."

"Brook...are you sure no one has followed or watched you? I don't think you know Harris like I do."

"That's where you're wrong...I know he's an asshole, but the difference between you and me is, I'm not afraid of him."

"Either way, I am so glad to see you and that you are here," Chelsea says with a warm embrace.

Brooklyn's embrace weakens, and the sound that comes from her mouth and directly into Chelsea's ear is many whispering voices, and as she pulls away, there is a look of death on her face with blood pouring down from her head. Her eyes speak, what her voice cannot as they look past Chelsea. Chelsea slowly turns to look in the direction that Brooklyn is looking. Seeing nothing, she turns and looks back at Brooklyn and sees a lump in the floor that continues to grow to the height of her own and taking shape and features of Harris. As she begins to approach Brooklyn, she grabs Chelsea with bloody hands, she opens her mouth to speak, and again, the only thing she hears is the many whispering voices, and she can barely make out Brooklyn's voice among the others. Even though he is still a few feet away, his hand reaches out, grabbing her by the neck, pulling her towards him. She feels the tips of her toes burning as they drag across the carpet.

"You're dead!" Harris yells in her face as the words echo deep into her ears repeatedly as she tries to pull herself away. The more she fights back, the louder his voice sounds and begins to ring in her ears.

Chelsea wakes up to the sound of the telephone
ringing and fear racing in her heart as she realizes it was all just another nightmare.

"Hello." She answers the phone groggily.
"Chelsea? Babe!"
"Yes."
"Are you alright?"
"Sure. Why would you ask that?"
"I've been trying to reach you, and you haven't returned my calls."
"Oh, I'm sorry, Ron. I was out back, raking leaves earlier, and when I came in, I just laid down for a nap."
"After what you told me what happened to Brooklyn, I was concerned when I didn't hear back. I had made up my mind that if you didn't answer this time I was coming over."
"Sorry, babe; I was just so worn out and tired. I'm really having a hard time with everything that's happened." She says, looking at the clock and through the curtains in the

dining room and finds that its now dusk.

"Would you like me to come over or are you going back up to the hospital?"

"You're sweet. I just don't think I would be very good company because my mind seems to be only on one thing."

"I understand. If you change your mind or just need an ear to bend, give me a call."

"I promise I will."

"Alright; I'll let you finish napping."

"Thanks for checking on me."

"You're my baby. I will always look after my baby."

"Thanks. I'll talk to you later." She says before hanging up and roll over on her side to close her eyes once again.

The moment she closes her eyes, she feels a strong presence of someone or something standing behind her, right at the bedroom door but the fear inside her will only give her enough courage to open her eyes. The presence grows stronger as she tries to gather the wherewithal to turn around, but the feeling of it seems to be coming closer to her...as if it's right upon her, within arm's reach. She closes her eyes and takes a deep breath to slow the pounding fear in her heart, but as she exhales, the presence feels even closer. She feels the heat of breath upon her neck and the tip of a finger just barely stroking the fine hairs on her neck paralyzing her from head to toe.

She begins talking to herself; silently convincing herself that there is no one there and to turn around and prove it.

"Turn around Chelsea, turn around! There is nothing there." She silently coaxes herself.

With every word of confidence, she grows a little braver, and her feet become free of the paraplegic hold. She moves a toe. She moves her feet back and forth.

"Turn the fuck around Chelsea!" She silently yells at herself.

Finally, she gets up the nerve to turn her body towards the bedroom door with closed eyes. Slowly, she opens one eye and sees nothing but the bedroom door and wall, but the unwanted presence is still heavy in the room...right in front of her. She opens both eyes and peeks out the bedroom door and straight ahead, right through the dining room and at the dining room window is a man's face boldly staring directly into her eyes as a smile grows upon their face. She screams a guttural scream causing the person to run off.

Still screaming, she scurries for the telephone and hastily dials nine-one-one but, she thinks twice about what she saw as she recalls the nightmare she had just before Ron called. She hangs up the phone, investigates the house, and grounds herself with a can of hairspray for a weapon. Making her way to the dining room, she peeks out the window where she believes she saw the face and sees nothing more than the front end of her car and the darkness beyond it.

She closes the drapes and proceeds to the front door where she walks towards the back yard with a dying flashlight that only seems to work when she hits it. While her attention is focused on keeping the flashlight lit, she hears something stir in the darkness, and that feeling of being watched returns. Quickly she jiggles and slaps the flashlight to shine in that direction, only to catch a small animal rustling through the leaves. With a sigh of relief, she quickly tries to open the back door to confirm that it is locked from the inside before she goes back to the front of the house. Being as cautious as possible, she looks behind her and all around the darkness and sees nothing.

"Boy, do I feel stupid. I almost called the cops for nothing." She chuckles to herself, feeling more confident as she goes into the kitchen for something cool to drink.

As she reaches into the cabinet for a glass, she glances out of the window and again sees the silhouette of a person in the gazebo.

"I wonder if that is just the way the roses are growing that makes it look as if someone is there?" She says to herself, before going to the back door to cup her hands around her eyes and pressing her forehead to look out. Seeing nothing, she turns on the backlight that shines right on the gazebo, and there stands a man in dark clothes, this time she sees a face. Their stare seems to pierce through her and reawaken her earlier fear. She's frozen again as the person grins and points directly at her.

Without a sound, she closes the curtains to the back door, grabs a butcher knife from the drawer, runs into the living room, and dials nine-one-one and sits frantically waiting for their arrival. She picks up the phone again to call Ron to keep her company until the police arrive.

"Hello." Ron answers.

"Hey, babe. It's me again."

"Well hey…I'm glad you called. Is everything all right? You sound a bit shaken."

"Well, I'm kind of hoping you would like to come over and keep me company."

"I would love to come over but, you still sound like something is wrong…so, what's going on?"

"A little while after I hung up with you, I saw someone looking through my window at me."

"What!! That's a while ago, Chelsea. You should have called the police and not me!"

"I have. They are on their way. I just wanted

to talk to you until they get here."

"I'm on my way there now!"

"No! Please just stay on the phone with me until they get here, please! I'm too afraid to hang up now."

"This sounds pretty bad Chels; there must be something you're not telling me."

"What do you mean? I told you, I just thought I saw someone in my window, that's all."

"I'm on my way!" He says before hanging up the phone, leaving her feeling abandoned and in danger.

Still clutching the knife, she slowly creeps towards the back door in the kitchen. She tries to look out the window of the back door again without having to cup her hands around her face or pressing her forehead against the window, but unfortunately, there is only her own reflection and background. There is no alternative...she must press her forehead against the glass She places her other hand against her face and window with the knife standing at attention beside her head and directly in front of her are a pair of eyes looking right back at her.

She screams and backs away, dropping the knife on the floor just as she hears banging at the front door.

"Police; Open the door!"

"Oh, thank God!" she runs to the front door, looks out the peephole confirming that it is the police and throws the door open.
Officer Taylor roams the house with his hand on his gun and holster. He returns from the kitchen with ease.

"Why were you screaming? There's no one here."

"I just saw someone in my backyard just as you were knocking!"

"I think who you saw was my partner, officer Miller checking the yard based on your call in." He replies, on his way to open the kitchen door to for his partner.

"Before I called, I saw someone out there and not only in my yard but, I swear they were looking through my dining room window. I know because when I screamed, they ran off."

"Is there anything different tonight from your previous call?"

"They were looking through my window right at me. After he ran off, I went into the kitchen and saw him in my gazebo, just like the night before."

"Alright." He responds while taking notes in his note pad as she speaks. "There's no one out there now but, because this is your second call with the same complaint, we'll have a car patrol the area throughout the night. That would discourage the predator from hanging around.

In the meantime, do you have a family member or friend that would stay the night with you?"

"I called someone while I was waiting for you guys to show up. They should be here shortly." She replies, just as she hears the officer on the porch questioning someone approaching the house. "Oh, that must be him now."

"What's going on?" Ron asks, approaching the house.

"Officer, I called him to come over. He's fine." She says.

"Chelsea, what happened?"

"It's alright now, Ron. I suppose whoever was out there ran off before the police could find them."

"Ms. Webber, you have our nonemergency number, and there will be an officer driving the neighborhood this evening. We'll leave you in the hands of your friend, so, lock up." The officer says, before closing the door behind him.

"Thank you, I will."

"Are you alright?" Ron asks, taking her into his arms.

"Yes, babe, I'm fine; just a little shook up."

"Is this the first time you've seen this person prowling around your house?"

"Umm, well...no."

"When was the other time?"

"The other night after you brought me home from dinner."

"What!? Why didn't you tell me?"

"I didn't want you to worry."

"Chelsea, I care about you, and I don't want anything to happen to you; especially since Brooklyn's beating. Don't ever do that again!"

"Do what? I didn't do anything."

"Don't ever keep things like that away from me again." He demands as he goes into the kitchen and looks out the back door and into the yard. "I don't know what I would do if something happened to you."

"I'm sorry." She replies on her way into the bedroom.

Before joining her in the bedroom, he ensures every window and door is locked.

"Promise you will never do that again?" He asks, sitting beside her on the bed.

"Do what?"

"Keep something this serious away from me. If there is any chance of you being in danger, I need to know about I can at least try to keep it from happening." He replies and kisses her forehead. "I will sleep on the sofa tonight. Do you have an extra blanket?"

"I'd rather have you beside me than out there."

He turns and looks at her, almost blushing. Finally, he would be able to feel the warmth of her body next to his, and the thought of waking up next to her put a smile on his face.

"You're sure?"
"Absolutely."
"Do you mind if I take a shower before bed?"
"Of course not. Please make yourself at home." She replies as she begins to dress for bed, making sure to keep her scar hidden from him.

*

Ron returns to the room to the sight of Chelsea lying on her side with her back facing him with closed eyes. He pulls back the covers and eases into bed beside her.

"Thank you for coming over, I really appreciate it." She turns to face him.

"I love you, Chelsea; that's why I'm here. I'm not here just because you asked me. I love being with you, and I want to be with you as much as possible."

She interrupts him with a kiss he gratefully accepts. He pulls her closer and kisses her more deeply. She presses her hands against his chest, pushing him away, nodding her head as she turns away from him.

"What? He asks. "Why did you stop?"

"I-I can't." She says, thinking about the scar.

"What's wrong babe; really? Is it because you don't feel the same for me that I do for you?" "Don't be silly; I love being with you."

"Chels, I didn't ask you that. I asked you if

you love me, the way that I love you."

"Of course, I love you."

"Then what's the problem with us expressing it physically?"

"Nothing. It's - just that - I'm embarrassed." She answers with tears flooding her eyes and her hand resting on her lower belly.

Although embarrassed, she wants to tell him the truth about her past relationship, and the truth about her marriage, the life he knew nothing of...nor the permanent mark in her life.

"Sweetheart, you are a beautiful woman, and you have nothing to be embarrassed about. I love you, and there is nothing that you can say or do that will change that."

"You're sweet Ron. I don't know what I would do without you."

A little frustrated with passionate desires and wanting to know the truth behind her fears, he props up his pillows, lay his head down and pulls her into his arms.

"Let's get some sleep, huh? We can talk tomorrow." He suggests with a kiss to her forehead.

She lays her head on his chest, feeling like she may lose him soon if she doesn't open up to him; but if she did, how would she even begin to tell him how horrible the marriage was or even explain why she stayed for so long, not to

mention that she's still married to him. Recalling his words, *"I will love you no matter what."*
She takes his hand in hers and guides it down to the lower part of her belly and strokes his fingers across the smooth and soft laceration of the letters her husband carved into her flesh for any man to see who she belongs to. He begins to venture on his own and continues to trace the letters as he pulls the covers back and lifts her nightgown for a better look.

"Is it a birthmark that you're embarrassed about?" He asks, looking sincerely into her eyes before actually looking at what he's touching.
He notices the tears pooling in her eyes and the fear of what he may think of her.
He pulls back and looks down at what he's touching. He's shocked, angry and embarrassed for her, but most of all, he is heartbroken for her.

"What is this, Chelsea? Is this someone's name? Are you telling me that you're already involved with someone?" He asks, sitting up in bed with his forehand resting in his hand.

"Ron, it's not what you think so, please don't get upset."

"Don't get upset?!? I can't believe you would let me get this involved with you and not tell me about the other man you're with. Damn!" He says and gets out of bed and paces the room.

She crawls to the foot of the bed after him.

"Ron, please listen to me. Please sit down and let me tell you my horror story." she pleads, grabbing his hand.

"Alright, I'm sitting. Go ahead and tell me why you let me believe that we had something together, when all along, you know who you wanted to be with." He says, sarcastically. "Just tell me why you felt you had to toy with my mind and have me falling for you more each day."

"First of all, there isn't anyone that I'd rather be with than you. You have been honest and caring and all the above. I know that if there's anything that I want or need, you are always there to see that I'm taken care of."

"Chelsea, if that's how you really feel, then why haven't you told me about him in the beginning?" He asks, pointing to the scar.

"Because I didn't want to lose you, and I thought if you knew the story behind this, you would definitely erase me from your memory." She answers. "Harris is my husband, and he carved the letters of his name on me because he thought I was thinking of cheating on him. It was his way of letting anyone that he thought I was sleeping with, know who I belonged to."

"Why don't you have it removed; or do you still hold some kind of torch for him?" he asks, sarcastically before getting up to pace the room again as many more questions boggle his mind. He stops when he hears her sobbing and sits back on the bed. "I'm sorry Chelsea. I shouldn't have said that. That was stupid of me. I'm sure you probably hate him for what he's done to you.

"I have too much shame behind it to find the courage to see a doctor about it." She heaves between words. "I would be more than happy to have this fixed somehow."

"Babe, I will be there with you if you can't do it alone." He says, taking her into his arms. "I will always be here for you."
He lays her down beside him and cuddles her snuggly in his arms. She feels secure and loved, something she hasn't felt in years. With her head resting on his chest, she slowly falls asleep to the rhythm of his heartbeat.

NOBODY'S PERFECT

It is six-thirty in the morning, and the sun is just about to rise when Chelsea wakes up; still cuddled in Ron's arms as if they didn't budge throughout the night. Carefully, she pulls back the covers and eases out of his slumbered embrace to start the coffee maker before taking a shower.

"It feels good to be in a loving relationship again." She thinks to herself, leaving the bathroom as she watches him sleeping. She wraps herself in her bathrobe as she proceeds to the kitchen to make breakfast.

*

The smell of food cooking and coffee brewing wakes Ron. He takes a shower, dries off, wraps a towel around his waist and greets her in the kitchen with a hug from behind. He kisses the back of her neck and shoulders. She closes her eyes and absorbs the sweetness that she thought she once had with her husband.

"How are you doing this morning, sweetheart?" he asks.

"I'm better now that the night is over, but I'm more afraid than I was in the beginning because this is the second time this person has been in my yard and this time, he was bold enough to look through my windows."

"What? You didn't tell me that they were looking through your windows at you. That's it! There is no way I'm leaving you here alone! Now, I'll either stay here with you or you are coming to stay with me until this person is caught!"

"Ron, I'm sure I'll be alright here at home. Besides, I'm not going to have some complete stranger run me from my own home, and that's final!"

"Fine. I'm going home to grab a few necessities and come back." He says, storming out of the kitchen and back to the bedroom before she can even respond, but she's following closely behind him.

She walks into the room, where he rips the towel from his body and reaches for his jeans and without a second thought, she gets closer to him. Taking his hand in hers, she goes in for a kiss. He attentively responds to her advancement, slowly tugging on the belt of her bathrobe then, eases his hands into her robe and down to her buttocks. She pulls him in closer, embracing him tightly and stroking his back, buttocks and even makes her way to attentive manhood. He gently caresses his way to her breast, where he begins to heighten her desire to feel him inside her. She moans with passion and desire that feeds his sexual senses, the signs that she wants him and that he is doing everything right.

He kisses from ear to neck, neck to shoulder, shoulder to breast, and from the breast down to the gentle parts of her inner thighs.

"Are you sure you want this?" he asks on bended knee looking up at her as he avoids looking at the offensive scar on her belly.

"I...I'm ready." She answers with closed eyes and a melting heart.

He removes her robe completely and guides her onto the bed where he continues to lavish kisses from her mouth while caressing every neglected inch of her body. Gradually, he kisses his way southward again, avoiding the scar on her belly; he kisses her inner thighs where he can feel the warmth of her precious moist flower near his face. Warm chills of excitement embrace her. The peaks of her breast stand at attention as she moans for more. He savors her flower as he reaches up for her hands and interlock fingers with her. She is in a fervent stupor, caught up in the pleasures of something she has not felt in years.

"Oh my...I don't want this to end." She moans.

He continues until he feels the throb of her clit on his tongue. He then kisses his way back upward and gives each breast a bit of attention as he eases his erect soldier inside her, causing her to gasp in pleasure.

"Chelsea...baby. I love you so much." He whispers in her ear as he continues to make love to her, kissing her face and mouth until they both reach their climax together.

"I love you too." She replies.

As they lay there cuddled, Ron kisses her on her forehead and proclaims his love for her again.

"I'm going to go home and pack a few things. I don't want you staying here alone as long as there is someone looking in your windows and lurking around your house."

"You know you don't have to do that, Ron. I will be perfectly fine here alone."

"That may true, but I would feel much better knowing what's going on when it happens and be here for you if it does happen. Would you like to come with me?"

"Well, if you don't mind, I'd like to go see Brooklyn until you get back."

"Babe, would you like me to go with you?"

"No. Thanks for the offer but, if I'm going to have you with me another night, I'd rather you gather your things." She replies with a kiss.

"I'm pleased that you're looking forward to it." He says with a smile before getting out of bed.

"Oh, I should probably give you a key in case I'm not back from the hospital by the time

you come back." She says, getting out of bed, wrapping her robe around her.
She goes behind the bar where the spare is kept.
"You don't have to do that Chels, I can wait until you get back."
"I want you to have it. Please."
"Alright; I'll see you tonight." He says on his way out the front door.
She takes advantage of the time alone to go upstairs and take care of some things so she won't have to make any trips while he's visiting.

***

On his way home, he reflects on his past and ex-fiancée Nichole.

It was two and a half years ago in January that he met her, but it was the days and months thereafter that he learned so much more about her that he thought, he
could tolerate. After a while, those things became intolerable, or she had some kind of justification for them.
He recalls a time when he should have started going with his gut feelings other than accepting her explanations and reasons for some of the things that had happened. Moreover, one of them was when she had given a party at her apartment before they had gotten a place together, and the guests that attended were of unexpected sexual preferences. Although that didn't bother him as much as catching her having sex with another

woman and a man.

"What in the hell is going on, Ann?"

"Come on, baby, join the fun," Nichole replied, rather nonchalantly.

"You have a house full of guests, and you're in here fucking a woman. Is this what you want? A woman?"

"No, baby. I want you. We're just having some fun." She explained as she got out of bed to approach him.

"You're stoned! Get the fuck out of my face!" He replied, then pushed her back onto the bed and stormed out of the room and out the apartment.

The following morning, Nichole was on the phone, begging for his forgiveness and promising to never smoke marijuana again. Only a month later, did he let himself into her apartment and found her in an argument with a friend. Nichole was on top of the woman slapping her in the face. "I'll kick your ass if I find out this shit to be true!"

Her explanation for that instance was that the woman was talking trash behind her back. After that, their relationship seemed to improve and thrive.

A year later, Ron and Nichole were to be married on New Year's Eve and everything was planned and going smoothly.

Ron stood at the altar, waiting for his bride

to come down the aisle. His family waiting patiently; some disappointed that he was marrying her, and some were happy for him. As the music began, queueing the bride to come down the aisle, everyone stood and looked in her direction. She was beautiful, as was her wedding gown.

The ceremony began; the minister spoke the words of vows and expectations.

"Whoever thinks these two should not be married, speak now, or forever hold your peace."

"I have something to say." A woman's voice comes behind.

"And who are you?" asked the minister.

"I am her lover of eight years, and she doesn't love him. She's just doing this to cover up our relationship." Says the woman Ron caught Nichole fighting with at her apartment. "And I'm sorry, Ann, but I don't want to share you to save face with society. I want it to be just us. I'm sorry for being with Gerald. It was a mistake. I just wanted you to know what it was like for me to see you with Ron as a couple as if I didn't mean anything to you at all. So, please don't do this. I love you so much, and it'll never happen again if it can be just you and I."

Ron, along with most of his family and friends, were shocked. Enraged and embarrassed; it was all he could do to keep himself from putting his hands around her neck and strangling her.

"Oh my god! I am sorry, Ron. She is right." Antionette said when she looked at him.

"You bitch!" he said, pushing her to the floor and climbing on her trying to choke her. Everyone in the church was on their feet trying to get closer to the attack and pull him off her. It took six men to get him off Nichole that day and, when she was finally pulled up from the floor, there was blood coming from her nose, and her face was pale from lack of blood to the brain. Unfortunately, his troubles didn't really start until after the church brawl. When she came back to the house that they bought together to get most of her things, he beat her so bad that it took two weeks to look like herself again. He was arrested and charged with assault and battery. That was the first and only time he had ever put his hands on a woman or felt like he could have killed anyone. He wasn't proud of what he did, and he actually apologized for losing his cool like that. He couldn't believe how much damage he had caused or that he was even capable of it. To this very day, he is still ashamed of his loss of control, and he had never been as humiliated in his whole life as he was the day of his wedding.

*

Two miles down the road, he begins thinking about this morning with Chelsea and how good he feels when he's with her putting a smile to his face. He smiles again, but this time at himself for growing an erection from the very thought of her.

He makes a few stops before going home to get the necessities. He stops at a jewelry store and then a pet shop where he buys a puppy, Bouvier. He purchases everything from the carrying cage to food and toys.

While the puppy is placed in the carrier, he looks at his watch and realizes he's been gone longer than he anticipated. On his drive back to Chelsea's house, he coos and talks to the puppy that is crying to be picked up or taken out of the carrier.

"Hey, pretty girl! You're going to have a very beautiful new owner, and she is going to adore you There is a great big yard for you to run wild in...you're going to love it."

***

Since Chelsea's last call to the police, Officer Miller has been watching her house with a personal interest. Just a couple of houses away, dressed in civilian apparel, officer Miller is sitting in his car thumbing through his notepad and jotting down his findings of Chelsea and Ron. He starts up his engine and heads down the road.

"How the fuck did I get myself into this shit?" he says to himself. "It's too late to back out now."

Officer Miller pulls into the parking lot of a Holiday Inn only two miles away from Chelsea's home and casually walks through the lobby and to the elevator. He knocks on the door of a room where a woman asks him to identify himself.

"It's me, Mike."

Officer Miller enters the room to the site of Harris sitting at the table with another cop from the force, laughing about how well their setup is working out for them. Mike signals with his hand for Harris to come out into the hallway with him. They close the door halfway.

"What's up?" Harris asks.

"I think that it's time to get to the point of this 'scaring game' we're playing with your wife," Mike replies.

"Oh? What's the status?"

"Well for starters, she's afraid enough to have him stay the night with her."

"I'll take care of that. As a matter of fact, I can kill two birds with one stone." Harris answers, stroking his beard.

"What are you talking about?"

"I'm talking about your partner in there. He seems to be on the up-and-up about working with us, but I need some proof that he won't sell out when this starts getting heavy because it will get pretty heavy."

"Why? Didn't he pull through last night at the house?"

"Yeah, but that wasn't shit. That was child's play. I need him to prove his worth on a much higher level."

"So, you're talking about paying more, right?"

"Of course."

"So, what do you mean about 'two birds with one stone'?"

"It's time to get rid of her new friend, and as an initiation to our plan, your partner Eddie will be the one to knock him off. If he does, then there's no problem with kicking out some more Benjamin's for you two.

"Alright, fine with me," Mike says, before reentering the room.

Eddie is sitting at the table smoking a cigarette waiting for instruction on their next move with Harris' plan.

The woman that answered the door is preparing to leave.

"If my services are complete, I'll take my money now and leave you men to your business."

"How much?" Harris asks as he reaches for his wallet.

"Five hundred." The woman replies.

"So, what's up?" Eddie asks as the woman leaves the room.

"Alright, this is what's going down for tonight;" Harris starts. "Mike, I want you to watch Chelsea's house. Call me when or if she leaves. Eddie, I need you to follow her friend, and when the opportunity presents itself, I need you to take him out."

Eddie looks over at Mike wondering if Harris is facetious. But there is no response from Mike, not even eye contact.

"Okay, so all I have to do is scare him."

"What the hell are you talking about 'scare him'? This, not a damn game, Ed! I want him dead. Now if you don't think you can handle that, then you need to be taken care of with the same bullet he'll be getting. Therefore, you had better come correct right now! Are you in, or are you dead?"

Although Eddie is known for abusing his authority as a police officer, he has never killed anyone and is far from wanting to go to jail for life over someone else's domestic issues. Almost too afraid to answer, he doesn't answer quick enough for Harris as he realizes how serious his request is.

"Well, damn man, you don't need to threaten me. The shit will get done...no problem." Eddie replies.

"Good. As soon as I get the call from you, I'll be on my way to meet you at her house. Eddie, I want you to bring something back to ensure the job is done."

"What do you want? His head on a platter?"

"If you can manage it, smartass! Be a little less creative than that." Harris responds. "Now, if I'm not here, then I'll be at Chelsea's or on my way there."

***

While at the hospital, still heartbroken over her condition, Chelsea sits in a chair beside Brooklyn, gently holding her hand. Although she appears to be sleeping peacefully, she is subconsciously in terror.

Brooklyn walks through the dining room of Chelsea's house, calling out her name. After checking every room in the house, she walks into Chelsea's bedroom beginning to think that she isn't home but, when she sees the door to the upstairs ajar, a sick feeling settles in the pit of her stomach knowing that Chelsea would never leave this door unlocked, let alone opened.

"Chelsea, are you up there?" Brooklyn calls. There is no response but a thump on the floor above her. Her heart beats faster as the fear of something wrong fills her soul. She slowly makes her way upstairs as quietly as possible. As the room above comes into view, she hears whispers. Peeking through the banister bars, she finds Chelsea bound to a chair with her mouth-taped shut as Harris paces the floor in front of her wielding a knife. He is chanting something, but she can't make out what he's saying.

Without taking another step but merely standing on her toes to get a better look, she is able to see the fear and pleas for help in Chelsea's eyes as tears fall from her face down to the floor into pools of blood.

"He's going to kill me, Brook!" Is what she sees in Chelsea's eyes. "Please, help me!"

Frozen with fear and helplessness, Brooklyn, grabs the banister rails and with all her might, she screams for Harris to leave her alone but, her screams fall silent as the sound never leaves her voice box. She tries to scream even louder as she gripping the rails tighter.

Chelsea feels Brooklyn squeezing her hand, not knowing that she is in the middle of a nightmare. She stands and taps Brooklyn on the shoulder as her grip gets tighter until she becomes stronger than Chelsea. Not wanting to hurt her, she uses her other hand to pry Brooklyn's fingers away. As she frees herself, Brooklyn opens her eyes in terror, trying to yell out Chelsea's name with only a loud mutter.

"Wake up, Brook! It's just a dream sweetie. I'm here!"

"Mmm, umm, umm!"

"What is it, Brook? What are you trying to say? Do you remember what happened to you?" "Mmm, uumm, ah!"

"What's this?" Chelsea asks, noticing a gauze on her forearm. "Were you cut too?"

Brooklyn tries with all her might to speak words that Chelsea could understand, but nothing makes sense. She somewhat understands what is being said to her, but it is just not as easy to respond.
Chelsea manages to get her calm again just before a nurse comes in to check on her.
    "It is alright. It was just a bad dream. You are safe here."

EVIL DOES...

Chelsea leaves the hospital, looking back in despair as she approaches her car. She can't seem to help thinking that none of this would have happened to Brooklyn if she did not start the argument the morning of her attack. Moreover, that justice will prevail on whoever did this to her.

Brooklyn slowly gets out of the bed to the bathroom pulling her I.V. hanger with her. As she approaches the mirror, she sees more gauzes like the one Chelsea mentioned. She peels back the bandage on her forearm, revealing a scar the size of a quarter with the impression of the letter 'A.' The cut is somewhat superficial but enough to require bandaging but not stitches. Although here memory for speech is gone, fragments of her attack are vague. She removes another bandage on her chest that resembles an 'R.' As she continues to remove more bandages, the word "You will be my messenger." Echoes in her ears like a siren, but, before she can remove the other bandages, a nurse walks into the room.

"What in the world are you doing? Come on now, you know better than that! We need these to heal. Come back to bed and let me give you some clean dressings for those." The nurse says,

calmly walking her back to her bed.
While Brooklyn is making her discovery, Ron is being followed but, his thoughts are solely on Chelsea.

After leaving the jewelers, he drives home for some of his toiletries. It isn't until he pulls up to his house, that he notices an unfamiliar car parked in front of his house, but he shrugs it off as a neighbor's guest and continues to take the puppy and his jewelry purchase in the house.

"You're a lucky girl!" Ron says to the pup. "I wonder what your new mommy is going to name you. We're just going to pick up a few things, then you get to meet her."

"Just keep cool man and open the door real slow and don't try anything brave," Eddie demands with a gun pressing to the back of Ron's neck.

Eddie pushes him inside and shuts the door behind them. He walks Ron through the house to make sure no one else is there waiting for him. He takes him to the basement, where within moments, a shot is fired, and then another. The sound barely echoes through the neighborhood while the puppy continues to bark.

***

The day becomes gloomy as the evening brings rain clouds and cool breezes on Chelsea's drive home from the hospital. Thoughts of Ron and their passionate moment this morning filling her mind and heart for more, she's anxious to find him there waiting for her.

"Ugh! Please don't start raining until I get until the house." She silently thinks.

She pulls into the driveway and sees that Ron has not returned, she takes the opportunity to make a candlelight dinner and have it ready upon his return. She kicks off her shoes at the door and takes them to the bedroom where she reminisces at the unmade bed that they made love this morning. With a smile on her face, she eagerly goes into the kitchen and starts preparing their meal.

In between marinating her meat and prepping her side dishes, she sets the dining room table with the usual setting but, not with the fine china she usually keeps on the table.

Once the meal is complete, she sets it on warm while she changes the linen on her bed. She lays a black silk negligee across the bed before getting into the shower.

Unable to hear the telephone ringing, Brooklyn is calling with the help of a nurse.

"I'm sorry sweetheart." The nurse says. "She must not be home yet. We can try her again later."

"Nnnnoooo...mmmm," Brooklyn replies, aggressively pulling and tearing her fresh gauges off.

"Don't get yourself worked up again. We have to keep your blood pressure in control." The nurse says, trying to keep her from pulling her gauges off. "It can cause more damage to your head injuries."

"Nnnnnooo, mmuu." Brooklyn shakes her head, fervently from side to side.

The nurse pushes the patience assistance button to get someone in to help her restrain her. Another nurse enters the room and injects Brooklyn with a sedative to quickly calm her down.

***

The plan is in effect as darkness falls. The keys are passed to Harris from Eddie, along with the engagement ring to prove that the task of taking out Ron is complete.

"Is it done?" Harris asks.

"Here is the proof." Eddie points out the blood on the jewelry box.

"No traces back to me, right?"

"Not a one."

"Perfect," Harris replies, then pulls an envelope full of money out of his inner breast pocket and slaps it into Eddie's hand. "You're excused."

Harris lets himself in the house as her answering matching picks up another missed call. He lights the candles and seats himself at the head of the dining table, waiting patiently for her to enter. His anger rises from the sight of the diamond ring that was intended for her by another. He closes his hand tightly around the object and shoves it into his pocket when he hears her getting out of the shower.

After drying off and applying lotion and perfume, Chelsea sees the glow from the lighted candles in the dining room and eagerly puts the negligee on.

"Hello, beautiful." Harris's voice resonates in the room.

Paralyzed with fear, her happy heart now pounds painfully against her breastbone as if it will beat right out of her chest. The voice alone says so many evil things, even with the sweetest words.

He slowly stands and walks towards her. He runs his finger down the side of her face, causing her to flinch. Although handsome, the candlelight accentuates the true monster that he is.

"H-h-how, did you get into my house?" She asks nervously.

"I have a key, of course." He replies, holding out his hand displaying the key. "Now, get your things, Chelsea."

"Harris, where did you get that key?"

"That's irrelevant, but since you act like you can't live without an answer, then I'll tell you; I got it from your boyfriend today after I knocked him off. I should kill your ass for messing around while we're still married. Did you tell him that you're still married?"

"Yes." She lies.

"Really? So, you're telling me he was planning on asking you to marry him despite the fact that you told him that we're still married?" He asks through clenched teeth displaying the diamond ring Eddie handed to him.

"What is this?"

"This is something he apparently bought for you today."

"No...Harris, what did you do?"

"Ha, what do you think I did?" He chuckles. "Now, get your shit, Chelsea. It's time to come home."

"No, Harris. Why don't you just give me a divorce and let me live my life?"

"Your life! Your life is nothing without me, and as I told you before, I will kill you before leaving you. You're lucky I'm not going to kill you for sneaking out and running away like that. I told you that I would find you if you ever left me." He says with a backhand slap to her face. "And that word 'divorce' is not to be heard falling from your lips again."

Tears fill her eyes, and even though she doesn't want him to see her cry, she can't help thinking something terrible has happened to Ron and blaming herself for whatever harm may have come to him.

"Why can't we just be adults about this? We just made a mistake in getting-"

"You really want to divorce me?" he interrupts. "We made a vow to love, honor, cherish until 'death do us part.' You notice how death is the only way out. So, are you sure that is something you want from me?" He asks, facetiously as he reaches for the switchblade he keeps attached to his belt; the very knife that he marked her with. He holds her by the waist and pulls her in close, placing the knife at her throat as he forces a kiss on her mouth.

"Now, are you sure this is what you want?" He asks.

"No, not like this. If I come back with you-"

"There's no 'if' you come back, you are coming back with me." He interrupts.

"When we get home, can we at least try a marriage counselor? And see them as a married couple? Not just me?"

"Is that going to make you feel better? If I say yes, are you going to stop all this whining and pack your shit?" He asks, putting his knife away.

"Yes, if you'll go with me." She says softly, taking his hand in hers. "Please."

"Well, we've already made a good start; I don't see why we couldn't see a therapist."

"What do you mean we made a good start?" She asks.

He pulls out a chair for her at the table, and she takes a seat. He stands behind her, places his hands on her shoulders, and squeezes firmly.

"For starters, we got your boyfriend out of the way."

"I don't have a boyfriend, Harris."

"Don't lie to me, Chelsea. I thought you wanted to start out on the right foot here."

"He's just a friend Harris. A very good friend of mine that is all."

"Maybe that's how you felt, but I was told differently, or should I say, shown otherwise." He says, pulling the jewelry box for the ring from his pocket.

"Stop it, Harris, you've played too many games with me to believe what you're telling me about him."

"Oh, you think I'm playing with you?" He chuckles behind her. "Okay; let's play 'show and tell.' I told you my tale, now, let me show you." He slams the ring box on the table in front of her causing her to flinch and nearly jump from her seat.

"What's this for?" She asks opening the box and revealing a princess cut diamond solitaire. She does not want anything from him except his signature on a few pieces of paper.

"Open it and read his inscription."

She opens the box and reads the inscription as best as she can under the candlelight. *"I love you, Chelsea– Ronald"* it reads. Tears pool in her eyes knowing that Harris must have said something to Ron to run him away and now seeing how much he really cared for her and now he is gone, cuts her like a knife straight through the heart. She drops the ring on the table as she puts her head into her hands to hide the tears that at the edge of her eyes, taking a deep breath, she pushes back her hurt for Ron and secretly wipes away her broken heart and years of humiliation and replaces them with frustration, determination and above all...vengeance. When she raises her head and opens her eyes, it is as if she is a completely different person.

She stands and boldly walks into the kitchen as Harris stands in shock over her sudden assertiveness.

"Hold on. I haven't dismissed you yet and-"

"Look, I've had a long day, and I don't have time for your games, Harris." She interrupts as he follows closely behind her. "I'm hungry, and my dinner is almost ruined, so if you're going to eat with me, then have a seat."

She hands him the bottle of wine, corkscrew, and wine glasses.

"Well, I'm glad you coming around and understand who you belong to." He replies on his way to the dining room.

As he pours the wine and takes his seat at the head of the table again, he watches as she appears and disappears into the kitchen and back. While in the kitchen, she reaches into the cabinet where she keeps her prescription drugs and takes a bottle of sleeping pills to crush finely into his mashed potatoes. She graciously carries the plates out to the dining room and sets his plate in front of him and hers at her seat. She disappears into the kitchen once more, and while out of her sight, he replaces her dish with his. She returns with two glasses of water and takes her seat.

"Well, it's about time." He criticizes, taking the first bite. "Mm, mmm, this is good Beautiful. I knew there was something I missed about you."

"Really? So, are you telling me that someone else was taking care of your other needs?" She replies with a look in her eyes that would make the devil leave the room, but the remark does not faze him.

After dinner, Harris goes into the living room, gets comfortable on the sofa and starts flipping through the channels on the television while Chelsea is in the kitchen cleaning up the dinner dishes as she waits for the sleeping pills take effect. It isn't long before he starts to get heavy-eyed but trying to remain on guard as he faintly hears voices coming from the kitchen.

"Chelsea, who are you talking to?" he calls out while sipping his wine. "Crazy ass bitch." He says under his breath.

"Myself." She calls back. "You, prick." She says under her breath, remembering all the terror and abuse he has caused her.

"Hurry up and get your shit so we can go home."

*

By the time she finishes in the kitchen and dining room, Harris is in a solemn slumber. She makes every attempt to try to wake him, from pinching him to shoving him off the sofa. Once on the floor, she drags him by the feet into her bedroom where she retrieves the key to the upstairs from the false bottom jeweler box. Although heavy, his weight is no match to the vengeance growing inside her now.

She binds him to a twin-size bed in the room that she put a deadbolt on in anticipation of him finding her. She shoves a rag in his mouth, taping it shut by wrapping the tape around his head a couple of times. She mixes the drugs that she stole from his bowling bag the night she ran away; with paint thinner, gasoline, alcohol, iodine, and scrapes from the red phosphorus from a match, hydrochloric acid and, cooks it on an old hot plate that she found in the room the night she slept with her stillborn baby. The smell is horrific. He barely flinches to the pinch of the needle as she injects 10 ccs of her concoction.

Thirty minutes later, she comes downstairs, locks the door behind her, and replaces the key in her secret space. She turns off the television in the Livingroom before returning to her bedroom. She pushes her bed to the other side of the room, blocking the vanity and bathroom. She reaches behind the bar in the dining room and grabs a flashlight before pull pulling back the rug revealing a trap door that she opens and heads down into it. The flashlight shines as far as the fourth step down. At the base of the steps are three blue plastic crates stacked on top each other displaying used candles and a box of matches. She shines the flashlight a few feet ahead upon a door and goes inside. Despite the slight dank smell in the room, she closes the door behind her.

  The flashlight glows upon a wall with a cross-centered on it and beneath it is a small wooden box with a dozen of candle around it. As she lights each candle, her heart breaks all over again as he honors her beloved infant daughter and the unspoken promise she made, to make her father pay for her premature death. Her whimpering barely echoes the room with her tears glistening like diamonds in the candlelight while she strokes the tiny coffin. The devastation she felt the morning her daughter was born and died returns to her heart as if it just happened. With that, her hatred for him grows.

After saying a prayer, placing a kiss on the coffin from her mouth to hand, she returns upstairs and puts everything back in its place. Maniacally, she retraces her steps; from drugging Harris and hauling him up to her secret space that she has been preparing for him in anticipation of him finding her. She picks up the telephone and dials Ron's phone number.

"Come on, Ron, please pick up!" She thinks aloud as she looks at her watch and realizes how late it actually is but, there is no answer. "I'll try him in the morning."

She retires for the evening after a shower and a little television, but her slumber is disturbed with concern for Ron. Despite the concern for her lover, she somehow finds comfort in knowing that Harris is right where she needs him to be...at her mercy.

ENEMY OF MY ENEMY

It is seven in the morning, and Chelsea is awakened by a loud thump above her. Groggily she rubs her eyes and sits up in bed. The thump sounds again. She smiles a bit as she vaguely remembered last night, and who could be upstairs waiting for her.
She gets out of bed makes a pot of coffee and retrieves more sleeping pills that she mixes into a cup of coffee, and makes a small breakfast that she sets on a tray and takes upstairs with her, locking the door behind her as usual. As she climbs the stairs her alter personality Julia comes to the surface, and she is pleased to know it is clear that Harris is awake and quite pissed off and confused about how he became so vulnerable that she was able to bind him in such a way.

"What the fuck have you done to me?" Harris yells as she removes the tape and rag.

"You may want to start being a little nicer to me. I am bringing you some coffee and a bit to eat. I don't have to feed your ass, you know."

"How the hell am I supposed to eat if I'm tied up?"

"I was going to feed it to you but, since you want to continue to be an asshole, I'll just leave it here for you to look at and wish you could be

eating." She says, stirring the coffee.

"You fucking bitch! I'm going to fuck you up!"

"*I'd like to see you try.*" She replies as she stuffs the rag back in his mouth and tapes it. "*Who's the bitch now, bitch? Now you can just smell that good cup of coffee and breakfast.*" She says before leaving the room.

*

With no thoughts or regrets, she carries on with her day just like any other but, Ron is still heavy on her mind. She picks up the phone and dials his number only to get a busy signal.

"This doesn't make any sense," Chelsea says as Julia fades into the background. She rushes to get dressed. Without a thought of Harris, she leaves to go to Ron's house with hopes that he is alive and safe.

"*Ron, better be alright, or I swear I'll kill Harris!*" Julia silently whispers in the background of their mind as she drives one block closer to his house.

She pulls up to the front of his house with her heart pounding in her chest and a queasy feeling in her stomach when she sees his car. Despite the fact that she usually feels this way around him, this is different. The whole block seems to have a wicked silence and appearance to it. There is a deep feeling that there is something seriously wrong. She goes and knocks on the front door; there is no answer, but she can hear a dog barking. Surely, he'll come to the door with the warning from the dog but, there's nothing. She leaves the front door and goes around to the back of the house but, before she can even make it halfway there, a man dressed in torn jeans and a dirty shirt with his ungroomed hair approaches her.

"Are you looking for, Ronnie?" He asks.

"Yes, I am. I was just about to walk around back to see if he's there."

"He isn't home, I'm sorry to say."

"But his car is here."

"The EMS was here last night, and I saw them carry someone on a stretcher and carry them off to the hospital."

"What happened?"

"I'm not sure ma'am. Some people were saying that they heard gunshots yesterday evening, and shortly after, I saw the EMS."

"Do you know what hospital they took him to?"

"I don't know for sure, but I would assume it would be the closest to the area. Potomac hospital will be the closest from here if you want to try there first."

"Thank you so much." She says, before running off to her car and speeding down the street.

The thought of going home to kill Harris is first

on her mind, but the urgency of Ron's welfare is more pertinent. In her rush, she pulls up to Potomac Hospital's emergency entrance, jumps out of her car without closing the door or turning off the engine and runs inside.

"Excuse me, please!" She pushes through a couple in line for check-in. "I was told that my boyfriend may have been admitted here last night. Can you please check to see if he's still here?"

"I'm sorry ma'am but, you're going to have to wait your turn. So please step back."

"Whose car is this out here running with the door open?" A security guard calls out. "If you don't move the car now, you will be towed." "I'm coming." She replies, storming towards the entrance.

"You may park in the visitor's parking lot, ma'am."

"Thank you." She replies, getting back into her car with tears filling her eyes.

She takes a moment to calm down and try not to think the worst as she sits in the car, before reentering the hospital.

She returns to the lobby and takes a seat. With her legs crossed, she nervously shakes her hanging foot while she waits for the couple to finish checking in. No sooner they take their paperwork and find a seat, she is back at the reception desk.

"Can you please tell me if you have a patient that was brought in last night by the name of Ronald Thorn?" She asks urgently.

"Please calm down, ma'am. I'm looking it up now."

"Well?"

"There was no one by that name registered here last night."

"Are you sure? T-H-O-R-N!"

"I'm sorry ma'am there was not, nor is there a Ronald Thorn registered at this hospital from last night until now. Are you sure he was brought into this hospital?"

"No...I'm not sure what hospital he was taken to. I just assumed it would be the closest to where the incident occurred. Thank you for your time." She says before storming out and back to her car.

*

On the way home, she feels a very familiar emotion of loss and horror, of something being taken away from her far too soon. Tears fill her eyes to the point of blurred vision. Her head begins to throb with pain at the temples, and the more she tries to hold back crying, the more painful it is for her. She pulls off the road and hugs the steering wheel as if it were Ron in his hour of need. She cries his name aloud and beats the steering wheel with her fists.

It isn't long before her fear turns to hate and

vengeance once more for the person that seems to keep ruining the good in her life...Harris. Throwing the car in drive and pushing the gas to the floor, she speeds off heading back to her house with one clear thought in her mind, and that is to make Harris pay to the point of no end. With anger leading the way home, she barely notices blue lights in her rearview mirror and only pulls over when the siren sounds.

"Shit! What the fuck else can go wrong right now?!" She yells as she arises from the stress of seeing an officer walking up to her car.

"License and registration, please."

"Is there a problem, sir?"

"Yes. You were doing eighty-five miles an hour in a forty-five mile an hour zone. That is considered reckless driving."

"Really? I didn't realize I was going that fast."

"Wait, right here." He says, taking her credentials back to his car.

As Chelsea's alter watches the office walk away, she sees Brooklyn's mother driving in the opposite direction.

"*Oh God no!*" she thinks to herself, as they make eye contact, and Mrs. Brown makes a 'U' turn.

"Please watch your speed, Mrs. Webber." The officer says after handing her a three-hundred-dollar ticket and returning to his car.

"Is everything ok Chelsea?" Mrs. Brown pops her head into the car window.

"Oh, hi, Mrs. Brown, everything is fine. How have you been? I'm sorry I haven't called since the incident, but I'm still kind of absorbing it all."

"I understand baby. So am I. It's still so hard to think that anyone would want to hurt her."

"I know…I feel the same way. Well, I must be going home now. I'll be sure to call you later." "Well, I'm on my way to the mall to get something for Brook. Won't you come along? I could use the company."

"I would any other time, but there are some things I really need to take care of."

"Oh, please, Chelsea. It would be a great help to me with picking out a new outfit. You two have the same taste in clothing."

"Alright; But I insist on driving."

"Okay, but we don't have to rush." Mrs. Brown says with a smile.

"Park your car around the corner, and I'll follow you."

*

Mrs. Brown, drones on about her marriage, and how boring it has become over the years since Brooklyn moved out accompanied the entire drive to the mall.

"I never thought that I would think of my baby girl actually being my only best friend."

"I used to wonder if I would ever feel that way about a child of my own."

"What do you mean 'used to'? Sweetie, you're still young, and you still have time. I just hope you meet someone that has some kind of sanity about him, unlike Harris."

"I guess you're right."

"Of course, I am. Nevertheless, you're not getting any younger sweetie. You should be out there now looking for a good man."

The more Mrs. Brown talks, the more Julia's mind wonders the subject at hand...Harris and the abuse, Ronald and their new beginning and now...the possible tragic end. Suddenly a dark memory casts its shadow on her thoughts recalling their first year of marriage.

It's a Friday that Harris called from a business trip to check on Chelsea, and when he didn't get an answer, he made a call and changed his flight to leave for home immediately. The entire flight he was concerned about whom his wife was with and what she was doing. The more he thought about the possibilities, the more upset he became. Chelsea returns from the grocery store and is in the kitchen, putting away the food when she hears him come through the door. She looked at her watch and remembered that he was not due home until Sunday morning.

"Who's there?" She calls from the kitchen. She grabs a knife from the drawer and creeps

into the living room where she was surprised to see Harris setting his briefcase down beside the sofa. "Oh, honey, you scared me! I thought you were coming back on Sunday. What happened?"

"Where were you?" He asked quite perturbed.

"When?"

"I called you quite a few times today, and you didn't answer. So, where were you?"

"Oh. Brooklyn and I went out to the mall this afternoon, and from there, I went to the grocery store and just got back. Was something wrong?" She asked, on her way back into the kitchen to return the knife.

"You're telling me that you are just now getting home from the mall and grocery shopping?" He asked, looking at his watch. "It is eight-thirty! I've been calling you since one o'clock this afternoon, and you're telling me that you are just getting home!" He yells with a forceful push to her chest, nearly knocking her off her feet.

She stumbles back a bit into the living room. He pushes her again and even harder, where she falls and hits her head on the corner of the fireplace.

"Who were you with Chelsea?"

"I was with Brooklyn, Harris. I swear! You can call her and confirm that."

She stood up slowly, grabbing her head where she feels the warmth of her blood.

"You think I'm going to believe her? The two of you are like peas in a pod. I know that bitch will lie for you. The next time I call damn it, you better answer the damn phone!" He said, then stormed out the door to get his suitcase from the car.

She goes into the kitchen, makes a homemade icepack with a paper towel and cubes of ice and placed in on her injury. She grabbed her keys and purse and walked out the door without another word to him. She sped off down the street; not really knowing where she was going or where she should go. The silence in the car gave her time to ponder the event that just occurred. For the year that they have been married, he had never raised a hand to her so, she began to wonder...something must have gone wrong with his trip and that was the reason he was trying to reach her so impatiently.

She found herself in front of the Riverfront apartments at Brooklyn's place. Before getting out of the car, she tried to reason out his actions towards her. She thought he is stressed about his new case or his efforts of trying to make partner at the firm. She looked at her face in the rearview mirror and made minor adjustments to her make-up and left the now wet paper towel in the cup holder before she went up to Brooklyn's apartment.

"Dang, girl! You miss me already?" Brooklyn teased when she opened the door.

"No. I just thought maybe you wanted to play cards or something."

"Is something wrong with your memory? I told you at the mall that I was going out. I asked if you wanted to come, but you want to be Mrs. Happy Homemaker."

"Happy homemaker..." Chelsea said under her breath as she walked over to the window and stared out at the view of Canada, while Brooklyn went back into the bedroom to finish getting ready.

"So; did you change your mind? Are you coming out with me?" She called from the bedroom.

"No. I just totally forgot that you said you were going out. Who are you going with again?"

"Geez Chels! Are you always this absent-minded, when your husband is out of town? I'm going out with Chiquita, Deidra, and Linda. We're going to the Summit and then to Elbows."

"Oh, yea." She replied, barely loud enough to be heard. The phone rang.

"Chels, would you answer that? It's probably one of the girls."

"Hello?"

"Hey, beautiful," Harris spoke. "I'm sorry about earlier. It's just that this new case is important to me, you know. There's a lot of pressure for me to win this case. You know I'm trying to make partner."

"I kind of thought about that afterward. I'm sorry for not being there for you when you needed me, but I want you to know that there is no one else but you."

"I'm sorry. I don't know why I think that so often. I do love you. You know that, right?"

"Of course."

"So, are you going to hang out with Brook for a while?"

"No. She is going out with some friends. I'm coming home now."

"If I'm not here when you get back, it's because I need to run to the office to pick up some things for this case."

"Okay. Would you like something special for dinner?"

"I don't want you to go out of your way. Whatever you feel like making is just fine with me."

"Okay. See you soon."

The faint sound of a car horn blowing brings Chelsea back to the present.

"Uh, oh, that was a close call, huh?" Mrs. Brown says in reaction to Chelsea, nearly sideswiping the car beside her. "Are you alright, Sweetie? Do you want me to drive back?"

"No. I'm sorry. My mind was somewhere else for a second."

"I can tell. You haven't answered any of my questions."

"I'm so sorry. What was your question?"

"I asked you; when was the last time you went to see Brook?"

"Oh. I was just there yesterday. She seems to be looking a little better. I just hope that they find the person or persons that have done this to her."

"Yes, me too. Her father hasn't been the same since the whole thing. That's his heart, you know."

"I know. It must be taking a toll on both of you, and I am so sorry. I must admit that we are blessed to still have her with us, and I pray it's just a matter of time that she'll be speaking properly again."

"I sure hope you're right. We pray on it every night."

"Me too, mom," Chelsea replies as they pull into the parking lot of Springfield mall, where they spend a couple of hours shopping.

Being out of the house and not rushing from one hospital to another, Chelsea's takes her mind off her troubles for a bit. The mall is cheerful and bright, calming all the emotions inside of her. They even stopped at the food court to get something to eat. The conversation dances around their childhood and adolescent years that Brook and Chelsea shared and how grateful they both are to still have each other in their lives.

"You are like a daughter to me Chelsea, and there is no one closer to Brook than you. You know she wouldn't let anyone say anything bad about you."

"I didn't know that. I do know she would do anything to keep anyone from hurting me, or her. We were peas in a pod back then."

"Well, you guys still are, aren't you?"

"Oh, of course. We're just older and have our own lives with boyfriends and husbands. You know?"

"Yes, I know."

"Although being in a relationship will never change the way we feel about each other; it's just that we have to split our time up with others that we love."

"You mean Harris?" Mrs. Brown asks.

"Yeah," Chelsea replies, looking away, embarrassingly.

"Hey, don't you worry about that, sweetheart. Brook knows what it's like to be in love, and she never spoke ill of you for what happened between the two of you."

"Thank you. It's just a regret that I've carried with me for a so long."

"You need not carry that burden. We all know that that situation was brought on by Harris. We know that wasn't something that you would have done willingly."

"Thank you so much."

"There's nothing to thank me for. You are like family, and we never turn family away. We knew Harris was abusive and possessive."

"Yeah...,"

"Hey; no need for those tears." Mrs. Brown says, wiping Chelsea's face with a paper napkin. "You know, there were many times Mr. Brown would get himself all in a huff to come and kick Harris's ass? It was just so funny to see him storming around the house and out the front door to go get you." She chuckles.

"Really? I'm so glad he didn't come. I wouldn't want anyone to get hurt." Chelsea responds, quite surprised. "I never would have thought Mr. Brown would be that angry."

"Well, I explained to him that if he went over there trying to take you away, that Harris could have him arrested for kidnapping. We knew you were too afraid to leave or press charges. But it all turned out for the better. You are no longer with him, and you are free."

"Oh boy, am I grateful for that and that you guys never treated me any different. I often thought about how stupid I was and felt you all felt the same way, but I never picked up that vibe from either of you. Thank you for that." Chelsea says with a hug and kiss.

"Oh! We better get going before we miss visiting hours!" Mrs. Brown exclaimed.

"You're right. I think we have enough time.

The hospital isn't that far. We'll be good to go if the traffic isn't bad."

"Is there ever a day that traffic is good in Virginia?" Mrs. Brown chuckled.

***

Upon their arrival to the hospital, Chelsea buys a little time alone to find out if Ron had been admitted there, by telling Mrs. Brown that she is going to buy something for Brooklyn from the gift shop. No sooner, she sees Mrs. Brown get on the elevator; she rushes over to the reception desk and asks about Ron. Disappointed with the response, she continues with the task at hand and buys flowers for Brooklyn.

As she leaves the gift shop, she sees Officer Edward Vadal and is surprised to see that he looks as if he had been in a bar fight. His eye is swollen shut, he has a cut lip, and his arm is in a splint. She approaches him regarding the prowler in her neighborhood that he responded to the night she called.

"Hi, officer Vadal. It's me, Chelsea Webber."

"Oh, yes. How are you?"

"I'm fine. I'm visiting a friend of mine here. And you?" She asks, trying not to be nosey.

"Oh, um..., I'm here following up on a case. I was just on my way out back to the station."

"I don't mean to pry, but what happened to you?"

"I...I really need to say something to-"
"What?"
"Come with me." He says, leading the way out of the hospital and towards the parking lot.
"What is it? What is going on? Does this have anything to do with the prowler I've been calling about?"
"Listen to me, Ms. Webber." He says covertly. "Someone is trying to hurt you, and they are willing to take out anyone that gets in their way to do it."
"What are you talking about, and how would you know this?"
"Ms. Webber; I'm telling you this in the strictest of confidence and because my hands are dirty...I want to make things right."
"What are you talking about? What happened that you're not telling me?"
Eddie reaches for a pen in his left chest pocket and writes his personal phone number on the back of his business card from the police station.
"I don't want to talk here about it. Call me at this number, and I'll fill you in on everything. I have to go now." He says before walking away briskly.
"What the hell is going on?" She calls out towards him as suspiciously scurries away.
She stares at the telephone number, wondering how much of what he is telling her, had to do

with Brooklyn or Ron. "What he could be talking about...is this the reason he's been beaten up?" she thinks silently on her way back into the hospital.

Chelsea struck with panic and concern as she gets off the elevator to the sight of Mrs. Brown leaning against the wall with her face in her hand crying. Stunned with the thought that the worst has happened to Brooklyn, she's paralyzed with fear. She loses her grip on the flowers she bought. Instinctively she runs to Mrs. Brown, trampling the flowers beneath her feet.

"What's wrong?"

"She had a stroke." Mrs. Brown cried.

"What! Where is the doctor?"

"The nurse went to get her. She said we can sit in the waiting room over there." She cries, pointing past the elevators.

"Come on. Let's go to the waiting room so that the doctor will know where to find us."

"Chelsea, I don't know how much more I can take.
I don't want to be here without my baby." She cries.

The wait seems forever as Chelsea paces back and forth, in and out of the room, nervously rubbing her hands around each other. Frustrated with not being able to solve the solution to Ron's whereabouts or well-being, she's rushed with emotions of the well-being of Brooklyn; and now with the vague story about someone out to hurt her from officer Vadal, she can't seem to have a moment alone enough to figure out any of this.

"Chelsea, please stop pacing! Somehow it makes me feel that things are going to be worse than they could be."

"I'm sorry, but things are worst!"

"Chelsea, please!"

"I'm sorry ma, but this was not a problem yesterday when I came to see her. Her eyes were open, and she was mobile! What in the hell is going on? Why are these things happening? Who did this to her?"

"Chelsea, please sit down or leave the room!" Mrs. Brown urges.

"Mrs. Brown?" Dr. Miller calls out as she enters the room.

"Yes!"

"Let me fill you in on your daughter's condition."

"Please do."

"What happened to her?" Chelsea interrupts.

"Let me first say that this is not uncommon for the type of head injury that she has." Dr. Miller explains calmly.

"I saw her yesterday, and she was fine. So, what happened?"

"Chelsea! Let the doctor talk!"

"She developed swelling on her brain late last night, which caused the blood to stop flowing to parts of her brain stem. This caused her stroke."

"Where is she now, and what happens next?" Mrs. Brown asks.

"We have her in a medically induced coma that will protect her brain and help reduce the swelling. We have her being monitored around the clock in ICU."

"I'd like to see her if you don't mind."

"Sure, Mrs. Brown. Take the elevator to the sixth floor and see the receptionist there."

"Thank you." She says as she heads for the elevator with Chelsea right beside her.

***

Seeing Brooklyn with wires and tubes, her body is a sight that Mrs. Brown takes very hard. Upon the sight of her daughter in a coma is more heartbreaking than seeing her with the injuries. She runs to her bedside and brakes down crying profusely.

"Oh, my baby girl! I'm here for you. I hope you can hear me. I love you more than anything on this planet. Please get better." She cries into the palms of Brooklyn's hand.

"I'm here too, Brook. I love you."

"Your daddy says, 'Hi.' He's sorry he hasn't come to visit you." She cries to Brooklyn. "He seems so strong and brave, but he just can't bear to see her like this." She says to Chelsea.

"I understand his position completely. I know it's hard when it's your own baby." Chelsea comments thinking of her own child. "I don't want to rush you, but I must get ready to leave soon."

"I know. I'm glad you came along. I don't know how I would manage on my own."

"I think you're doing just fine, and I'm more than happy to visit with you on a day that we plan together."

"That would be wonderful, Chels."

"Maybe tomorrow?"

"Wonderful. You hear that, sweetheart. We're coming back tomorrow." Mrs. Brown says with a kiss to Brooklyn's forehead and hand.

"See you tomorrow, sis. I love you." Chelsea says with a kiss to the cheek before leaving the room.

OPPORTUNITY KNOCKS

As soon as Chelsea walks in the house, she kicks off her shoes, reaches into her jacket pocket, pulling out its contents and tosses them on the dining table. Just before heading to the kitchen, she notices Officer Vadal's business card that he gave her at the hospital. Curious about the conversation they were having, she picks up the phone and calls him.

"Vadal." He answers

"This is Ms. Webber. I want to know who it is that you think is out to get me, and how long did you know about it?"

"Not over the phone. Can you meet me?"

"After what you told me at the hospital, how do I know that you're not setting me up?"

"Ms. Webber, I understand your suspicion, but did you see my face today?"

"Well, yes, I did. Are you telling me that whoever did that to your face is the same person that is after me?"

"Please! Not over the phone!"

"Fine; Where?"

"Arlington Cemetery. Take McPherson Drive to the Memorial Chapel gates."

"You're serious?"

"Yes."

"When?"

"How long will it take you to get there?"

"I can be there in twenty-five minutes."

"Perfect. Do not acknowledge me until we are around the tourist. I will come to you."

"Okay."

"Thank you. See you soon." Eddie says before hanging up.

Straight away, she grabs her keys and puts on her running shoes. She pauses for a moment with their hand on the doorknob; she turns around to get a small can of mace and a pocketknife.

"Just in case..." She says, walking out the door and locking it behind her.

***

By the time she gets to the cemetery, it is near closing. She gets out of the car and quickly scans her surroundings in an effort to find Officer Edward Vadal, but he is nowhere in sight. She precedes through the gate, despite the beauty of the autumn foliage, trees of orange, red and gold towering above the gravestones of a peaceful sight, she is more concerned about the danger that Eddie spoke of.

"Thank you for coming." Eddie says softly behind her. "Don't turn around. Go towards the crowd...I'll follow."

"You need to start telling me what is going on, and why aren't the police doing something about it?"

"There is a reason for that too." He says as they get closer to a crowd, with him following closely behind.

"I'm listening."

"They were told it was just kids in the neighborhood playing around and that it was nothing serious."

"Why were they told that, and by who?"

"Listen, I'm risking everything, including my life talking to you right now, let alone being seen with you. So, what I'm about to tell you, I need you to remain calm and nonchalant."

"Oh, shit...this doesn't sound good. As a matter of fact, this sounds like some crooked shit my husband used to pull back in Detroit."

"So, you're familiar with his M.O.?"

"You son of a bitch!" She says, between clenched teeth and under her breath as she turns towards him.

With this partial admittance, she is now on guard and scans her surroundings for his partner or anyone else that may have had something to do with stalking around her house.

"No...no just wait a second. I'm here to help you. I need you to understand something."

"What I understand Officer Vadal, is that I cannot trust you and you're a dirty fucking cop. That's what I understand." She says, pointing her finger in his bruised face.

"Wait! Please wait!"

"What is it? What can you possibly tell me that will make me trust you now?"

"I was set up too." He says, looking around the cemetery.

"Oh, ...so, you can't trust the bastard now?" She asks facetiously.

"Not just your husband, but my partner."

"Really? Now why is that and how will your realization help me at all?"

"They sent me out to kill your male friend, and when they found out that I didn't, this is what they did to me before threatening to kill me with my own gun and pin the crime on your friend."

"Oh, my god! Where is he? Is he alright?"

"He's fine. I told him to lay low for a while. I may have done some pretty dirty things and taken advantage of my authority but, I have never killed anyone...not even in the line of duty, and I wasn't about to start."

"So, what is it that you need to tell me?"

"I know that your husband intends on taking you back home with him, and I know to keep me silent, they both plan to put a hit on me."

"So, this meeting is more about saving your ass than mine."

"No. It's to save us both."

"How is that?"

"I know your husband came to you last night because we were told to let him know when you got home. Now, I don't know where or what he is up to now because I haven't seen him since."

"And?"

"I don't know how you feel about him or if you plan on going back with him, but I want you to know that I have connections if you want to get back at him."

"What are you talking about? Get back at him how? Moreover, what are you going to be doing? Notifying the police of my every step?"

"No. I've given my two weeks' notice, and I'm moving out to the west coast."

"Why are you trying to help me? Why couldn't you be a good cop from the beginning?"

"I needed the money, and he made an offer I couldn't refuse, only I didn't follow through with the request."

"Well, it seems to me that you realize who you were fucking with. My husband is the spawn of Satan, and you can best believe that if you think you're going to run away with his money without completing a job, ...he will find you."

"I have to hope for the best. I have a wife and two kids. I have to move them out of harm's way."

"What are these connections you're offering me?"

"I know some people that know how to make people disappear."

"Are these the same people that are helping you?"

"Yes."

"I appreciate your help, but I'm not running from my husband anymore. I am tired of running and hiding. If he finds his way back to me, he'll regret every minute in my presence."

"What are you going to do? The man is seriously crazy!"

"Do you know where I can get my hands on some drugs?"

"What? What kind of drugs?"

"I'm looking for something specific."

"Like what?"

"I'm looking for something called 'Devil's Breath.' Have you heard of it?"

"Yes. I can get my hands on some." He answers.
"How do you know about that drug? You know You should be extremely careful when handling it. Wear gloves and do not inhale the scent."

"Can you bring it to me this evening?"

"Can I leave it, someplace? I don't want to be seen back at your house. I know they are probably looking for me."

"Thanks. Do you know where Accotink Park is?"

"The park in Springfield, off Hemming Avenue?"

"Yes, that's the one. Once you enter the park, park your car near the train's trestle, and place it under a stone next to the trestle's structure."

"I can do that."

"Can you do it tonight?" She asks, looking around the cemetery.

"Yes."

"Good. You've helped me more than you know."

"I hope you stay safe, and I know there is no need in me telling you to be careful; you were married to the man after all." He says, somewhat sadly.

"I don't know what caused you to have a "come to Jesus" and go straight, but I appreciate your warning."

"You will not see or hear from me again."

"What about your partner?"

"What do you mean?"

"Will I be seeing him?"

"Only if your husband contacts him. I need to go now. I'll have the package at Accotink by four or four-thirty." He says, walking away towards Memorial Drive to catch the metro.

It was only for a second that Chelsea wondered why he did not drive. Her mind immediately turns to Ron and hope he would contact her soon. One thing is for sure, and that is, she is sure to take all her anguish out on Harris, and she is anxious to get home to do it.

*

She takes her time walking back to her car, enjoying the peaceful scenery, the beauty of fall colors and those resting beneath it and thinking with a wicked grin of Harris resting beneath her feet. But not in a lovely place like this...no, no he deserves something far less cared for...maybe even in a hole not deep enough to cover him, where wild animals can dig him up and eat off of him and drag his sorry ass body around for other animals and birds to feed off ofhim.

"*Poor animals; They don't deserve to be treated that way; they should have better food to eat than that evil bastard...too bad, he can't be buried into the core of the Earth.*" She thinks aloud to herself.

The drive home is more pleasant than she started out this morning. With the reassurance that Ron is safe and alive and the thought of receiving her special package this evening, she is anxious to get home and relax before tending to Harris. As she crosses the Fourteenth Street Bridge, she notes the time, and that Accotink will be closing soon, so instead of going home, she heads straight for the park.

As dusk falls, she reaches the narrow road that leads into the park. The trees are full with autumn colors and an occasional gleam of light piercing through the leaves of the trees, casting shadows on the car and road as she comes closer to the parking area near the trestle. With the trestle in view, her anticipation grows, and despite the few people around, she has no qualms about pretending to find something near it. She even returns the greeting gestures that are cast her way.

She plants herself at the trestle resting her back against its structure where she sees what looks like a shiny blue wrapper sticking out from under a rock. She pulls a book out of her purse and places her book down on top of it for a second to appear to get comfortable to read.

"Hey, lady, the park is about to close. You may want to pack up and get ready to leave."

"Oh, thank you so much." She replies, grabbing her book and package, placing them in her purse before heading to her car. "I totally lost track of the day." She calls out.

On the way, home, she could not wipe away the sinister grin on her face as she thinks about what she has planned for Harris.

*

She takes her little package and makes her way upstairs, locking the door behind her as usual. She enters the room to the sight and smell of Harris. She has not allowed him any bathroom privileges and does not intend to.

"Have you been behaving yourself? Oh my god! You smell like shit! No matter; I still have a nice surprise for you." She says, slowly approaching him waving the special package Vadal left for her at the park. "You're going to enjoy this…I'm sure."

She carefully opens the package in his view. She reveals the grayish powdery substance and a syringe. Harris begins to shake his head back and forth fervently.

"Harris! Cut that out! You know I wouldn't give you something that isn't potent!" She says, preparing to cook a small amount in a silver spoon. The odor on top of his unattended bodily functions become more than she can bear. She opens a window for some form of relief.

Wanting to make eye contact with Chelsea, in hopes of finding some form of empathy or reprieve, he finds staring back at him something more bewitching and malevolent than he had ever seen in her eyes before. From the look in her eyes alone, he silently begins to pray, knowing this may be his last day.

"I've never done this before, so I hope it's

not too much." She says, filling the syringe from the spoon. "Although, I have seen my uncle use on a number of occasions, and I don't think he filled it past this number five here."
She taps the syringe forcing the air bubbles to the top and gently presses the plunger, releasing the air and a few drops of the drug.
Harris begins to stir, while his muffled pleas are ignored.

"You know, I would tell you to calm down or be still, but you're actually showing me some pretty good veins so, by all means, continue to struggle. Oh, my Harris! That one in your neck looks good and juicy." She says as she approaches him. "Whether you are still or not, this is going in you, no matter how many times it takes. So, don't think that you are going to try to make this hard for me. I don't have any plans today. I have been looking forward to the opportunity to match all the shit you have done to me. No, no...let me rephrase that. I don't want to match it...I want to top it." She says, pushing down on the plunger.

*

Chelsea sits relaxing, smoking a cigarette watching him succumb to the effects of the drug as if she is watching a television show.

"That a boy. Just go with it. There is plenty more where that came from." She says with an evil smile, exhaling her last drag then stubbing the cigarette out on the flesh of his forearm before carefully putting away the stash and locking him into the room.

Elated, she nearly skips down the stairs, feeling as secure as she did the day, she left him.

Meeting of the Minds

The sun has set, and it is late afternoon, while Chelsea is sitting in the gazebo, relishing in all the things that she can do to Harris.

She hears a car entering her driveway and gets up to see who it is.

"Ron!" She yells with excitement, throwing her arms around him. "Are you alright? I've been trying to reach you and even went to your house. I was scared to death when your neighbor said he saw an ambulance in front of your house. What happened?"

"The long and short of it is somebody tried to rob me at gunpoint." He replies as they make their way into the house.

"Where?"

"At my home; the perp came up behind me as I was unlocking my door, with a gun to the back of my head and when I attempted to get the gun away from him, it fired. It ricocheted off something and went through his arm, and the second time it went off the bullet grazed his face. He still had a lot of fight in him after I finally knocked the gun out of his hand. We were fighting at the top of the stairs to the basement. I punched him in the face about four or five times before, he fell down the stairs. He didn't get up anymore after that. I just assumed he was dead and called the police."

"I am so sorry." She says, reaching out and grabs him around the neck, squeezing him tightly. "I was up this morning looking for you at every hospital that I drove by. But right now, I'm just thankful that you're here with me and alive."

"I'm good babe. After I left the police station, I stayed at my sister's house while they investigated my house."

"Investigate your house for what?"

"Because it was an armed robbery and a gun was fired; they considered it a crime scene."

"Why didn't you call me? I was worried, sick."

"Why were you worried?"

"I was expecting you to come back over, and when you didn't show up or return my calls, I thought something happened or, if I did something to upset you."

"I was on edge after the incident, and I would not have been in a pleasant mood at all. So, I just stayed at my sister's until I cooled my head enough to tell you everything that happened." He replies, taking her by the hand and leading her into the house where they sit on the sofa. "Are you ok?"

"I am now that I know you're alright." She answers with a passionate kiss.

"Mm. You must've really missed me."

"You have no idea." She replies.

"I had something to give to you but, unfortunately, it was lost in the robbery. The police may find it during their investigation of the house."

"What did you have for me?"

"Something nice, and if they can't find it, it can be replaced, so don't worry, you'll still get it."

"You're not going to tell me what it is? No matter; I am happier that you are alright, and here with me now."

"I missed you, babe. I hope you don't mind, but I would love a stiff drink." He says.

"Oh sure; what would you like?"

"Brandy if you have it."

"I do." She says, stepping behind the bar to retrieve a glass and the bottle of Domaine Boingneres. "Would you like some ice?"

"No, thanks, babe." He answers, as he gets in motion to sit in the lazy boy.

The telephone rings.

"Excuse me, Ron, I have to get this." She says, handing him his drink.

"Of course, go ahead."

While on the phone, Ron turns the television on low and waits patiently until she is done. Sipping on his Brandy, he eventually dozes off to sleep in the chair.

Chelsea hangs up the telephone, quietly goes

over to him and whispers in his ear.

"Do you want to stay the night with me?"

"Umm hmm" he mumbles.

"Come on and lay down in the bed, Ron." She says, pulling him to his feet after setting his glass on the table.

She leads him to the bedroom where she helps him undress and things begin to heat up, as one kiss leads to another and...other things.

***

It's midnight, and the moonlight casts shadows in the bedroom. The sound of crickets and frogs communicating in the night sounds almost sinister yet soothing. With the bedroom window, open, Chelsea can hear the leaves blowing in the wind. Regardless of the cool evening, she is feeling a little sweaty beneath the blankets. She throws the blanket off her, but before she can get back into that deep sleep, she is jolted awake by a tall, dark figure at the foot of the bed.

Frozen with fear, she cannot move and is too afraid to even blink. First, she thinks that Harris has set himself free and is planning to hurt her and Ron. "Harris?" She whispers. "What are you doing?"

The figure only seems to grow larger and not respond to her calling out. Her chest begins to pound with fright as the figure slowly hovers above her. She is not brave enough to nudge Ron, and she can only move her eyes to look around the room.

"You will never get away with this." *A deep raspy voice echoes above her, trembling the windows and nightstands. There is no face to this dark shadow as she feels the heat and stench of the breath upon her face.* "Just when you think it's all over, I'll be back for you. You are mine...you belong to me."

Finally, able to blink, the image and stench are gone. Now able to move again, Chelsea gets out of bed and goes into the bathroom. She wipes her forehead of sweat and combing through her hair with her fingers; she turns the light on and terrified by the sight of blood on her face, hands, and nightgown. She rushes back into the bedroom and immediately shakes Ron's shoulder. "Ron! Wake up! Wake up, please!" *She screams in distress.*

There is no movement or sound from him. She turns the light on finds his pillow saturated with blood as well as the sheets. She rolls him on to his back only to be petrified to find that his head is detached from his body. She screams to the top of her lungs, where she feels the force of the scream deep in her chest.

Chelsea wakes up trembling and sweating, panting as if there is not enough air in the room. She looks over at Ron sleeping peacefully beside her. Carefully, she pulls back the covers to make sure there is no blood on the pillow or him. Relieved, she takes a deep breath and kisses his face.

Now angered by the dream and at Harris, she retrieves her key to upstairs to pay him an unpleasant visit.

"You son of a bitch!" She says as she unlocks the door to his room, finding him fast asleep. She cracks open the window to cook up another dose of the Krokodil to inject into him. The cooking of the drug smells so bad that she hopes the smell does not linger down to the bedroom and wake Ron.

"What are you doing, Chelsea?" Harris asks groggily when she removes the tape from his mouth.

"Harris, I have never hated anyone in my entire life as much as I fucking hate you."

"What the hell did I do now?" He asks just before she rips the tape from his mouth.

"What didn't you do asshole? I hate you for who you are and who you pretended to be to get me to marry you. I hate you for the beatings, putting me down and all the sadistic shit you put me through that made me lose my baby, you fucking bastard! I want you to die...I want this shit to kill you. But I am looking forward to seeing the effects of what this drug does to your flesh and when I see that, you will be free to leave because, it won't be long after that, that you will die." She says injecting the drug concoction she created into the vein in his neck. "Now this is just a little more than what I gave you the first few times. I'd like to speed up this process of killing you if you know what I mean."

***

By dawn, Chelsea is still sound asleep when Ron wakes and sits up in bed. He cannot seem to take his eyes off the door that leads upstairs. With curiosity tugging at him, he gets out of bed and tries the doorknob, only to find it locked. He could swear that he heard voices in the middle of the night coming from beyond that door. He shrugs his shoulders and chalks it up to a vivid dream he must have had, then heads into the kitchen to make coffee and breakfast.

The telephone rings just as Ron reenters the bedroom with breakfast on a tray.

"Hello?" Chelsea answers groggily.

"Who in the world could be calling this early?" Ron asks.

"Sure, hold on a second." She says, handing the phone to Ron. "It's the police." Is this for me?" she asks about the breakfast.

"Hello, this is Ronald Thorn." He gives Chelsea, a nod, to answer her question. "Oh, that is great news, thank you for calling."

"What was that about?" Chelsea asks.

"They wanted me to know that I can go back into my house now and that they've gathered all of the evidence they need for the incident. I know there is going to be a hell of a mess to clean up." He says.

"I can come along and help with the cleaning if you like." She offers.

"I will not object to your generous offer." He says, on his way to take a shower.

"Are you going to have any of this delicious breakfast you made?"

"No, I'll just have a cup of coffee." He replies.

"Well, thank you for breakfast, sweetheart."

*

As they pulled into the driveway of Ron's house, Chelsea begins to feel a little uneasy about what she is about to see inside. Seeing the destruction upon the entrance of the house infuriates her more than she would have thought. To think that this is the result of Harris's attempt to kill Ron. There are small splatters of blood on the wall leading to the basement, a bullet hole on one side of the wall and an indentation the size and shape of a head on the opposite side of the wall.

"Oh, my God Ron!" I'm so glad you weren't seriously hurt." She comments, with thoughts on how to make Harris pay for these actions.

"Yeah, babe, me too."

He enters the kitchen for a bucket and cleaner with Chelsea following him. From her peripheral vision, she spots the turquoise Tiffany box on the basement floor, opened and empty. Quickly she reaches in her pocket tossing the ring down to the basement and carefully watches to see where it lands. The sound of it hitting the floor is drowned out by the sound of Ron filling the bucket with water and cleaner. The ring ricochets off the floor and to the right of the basement near the wet bar.

"Ron, I can clean the blood off the wall if you would like to start in the basement."

"You are a sweetheart. Let me get you some latex gloves. There is some cleaner under the sink there." He says on his way up the hallway to the linen closet for more supplies.

After filling the bucket with Lysol and water, Chelsea takes the bucket to the top of the basement stairs and begins to scrub the wall. For every little splatter of blood that she tries to clean the more, she considers getting rid of Harris sooner than she had planned. After all, it was merely for her pleasure to keep him around and make him suffer a long, painful death, but now that she has Ron safely back in her arms, there is no reason to keep him around any longer than need be.

"Hold that for me?" Ron stops to kiss Chelsea on her shoulder on his way to the basement.

"I may never let it go." She replies with a smile.

"You'll let it go in place of another." He says,

and then quickly gasps.

"What? What's wrong?" She drops the sponge in the bucket and begins to rush down after him.

"Nothing." He quickly lies as he spots the Tiffany ring box.

"Are you sure?"

"I'm positive. I just didn't realize how much of a mess we made during the struggle. You continue what you're doing, and I'll get started down here." He says, picking up the box, with eyes anxiously looking around for the ring.

He begins to sweep the floor of glass and dirt starting from the left side of the room as he continues to look for the ring.

"Ron?"

"Yeah, babe?" he replies in the distance.

"What are we going to do about the hole in the wall and that big dent?"

"When I'm done with the cleanup, I'll go to the home improvement store and get some spackling. That should be an easy fix...although; I don't know that I can say the same for that dent in the wall. I may have to call a handyman out to fix that."

*

They clean for two hours and as Chelsea retrieves the dustpan for Ron; he continues sweeping up the last bit of dirt and serendipitously sweeps the ring into the dustpan.

"Oh, thank God!" He says.

"What?" What happened?"

"Oh, nothing; I just found something I thought I lost."

"Well, what is it?" she asks, coming down the stairs to the basement. "Can I see it?"

"You're a nosey rosy, aren't you?" he says with a kiss. "I think we're all done down here. How does the wall look?"

"Aside from the hole and whoever head went through that wall, I think it looks good. At least most of the blood is gone. I think you may have to paint over it though. Dried blood isn't the easiest thing to clean."

"That's fine. I'm going to have to paint anyway once I get the walls fixed."

"Well, if we're all done, would you mind taking me home? I'd like to go see Brooklyn. You're more than welcome to come with me if you want."

"I appreciate the offer babe, but I'm not going to feel comfortable in my own house until I get it back in order. I don't want any memory of the incident staring me in my face when I come home or when you come to visit."

"I understand." She says with a kiss. "Hold that for me until you see me again...hopefully tonight?"

"I'll hold it for you, alright." He returns the

kiss. "Come-on. I'll drop you off on my way to the home improvement store."

When Ron drops Chelsea off, she gets right into her car instead of going into the house and heads off to the hospital.

Walking towards the hospital, an unusual warm breeze blows through her hair and softly across her face. Suddenly, she feels as if everything in the world is all right. She has her man back safe and unharmed and her ex at her mercy. All she needs now is to have her best friend back to normal, and she believes this too will come to fruition.

***

It is nearly 7:30 in the evening when Chelsea leaves Brooklyn's side to let her rest, and despite her pleasant farewell, her persona changes the moment she slips the key into the lock of her front door. The audacity of Harris trying to intimidate her by nearly killing the two people she loves infuriates her to no end.

Livid, she slams the front door so hard that one of the windows shook, causing it to crack. Seeing Ron's wall with a bullet hole and blood on it keeps flashing in her mind as she imagines the terror that Brooklyn must have gone through the night of her attack makes her wish that she could tear Harris in two with her bare hands. She storms through the living room and dining room straight for the bar and pours herself some tequila just to calm her. She takes a sip on her way to the living room catching a glimpse of herself in her vanity mirror as she passes her bedroom door. What catches her eye is her reflection sitting in front of the mirror staring back at her, signaling her to come near. In disbelief, she shuts her eyes and turns away but, when she opens her eyes, the reflection is the same...still fingering the motion for her to come near. She leans forward for a closer look, and when she leans back, she sees that her standing reflection is not holding her glass but, it's holding a lighted cigarette. Seeing these images of herself at one time startles her. Her glass falls from her hand, spilling on to the carpet. The sitting reflection continues to signal her to enter the room. As if hypnotized, she enters the room and takes a seat at the vanity with her reflections and stares into the mirror at them.

"*You know what?*" The smoking reflection Says Julia, the smoking reflection. "*You need to take your ass up there and kill him for the shit he's done to us.*"

"*He's not worth going to jail over, Julia.*" The sitting reflection responds. "*Killing him is just going to make matters worse for Chelsea so, that's not even an option. But you do need to go up there and let him know that you're not going to let him get away with the shit he did to our girl or your man for that matter. We understand that you're still afraid of him, which is why we took matters into our hands when the fucker showed up that night."*

"But what if he's loose and up there waiting to jump me?" Chelsea asks.

"Oh, I'm pretty sure he cannot get loose from the way I bound him." Says Julia, the smoking refection. "Billie here didn't want me to bind him but, I did it anyway. Hell, you're not going to give me a toy and then tell me that I can't play with it. Trust me, he's not going anywhere until you let him go."

"Shut up, Julia! We really need to teach him a lesson, but we don't have to kill the bastard." Says the sitting reflection. "Now come on...let's go upstairs."

While Chelsea stares into the mirror, the lighting around her slowly dims, her surroundings become shadowy as her reflections become inextricably one. Her head feels heavy, and even though she's sitting, she becomes off balance in her seat as she becomes alert again.

As Julia in her anger, she nearly rips the doorknob off, forgetting that it's always locked.

"*FUCK!*" she yells out loud in frustration for not being able to get to him fast enough.

Her yell awakens Harris's fear of what she may inflict on him now and, for what reason this time. Although his fear of treatment isn't as strong as his new addiction; to which he will endure anything for another hit. He hears the door to the stairs slam shut and locks. His heart begins to race with worry as he hears the door unlock to his room.

"That's it mutha fucka!" she says, lighting a cigarette. Her voice so ferocious, that if he weren't looking at her face, he would have thought she was someone else.

Immediately, she puts on a pair of latex gloves and prepares his next…maybe even his last fix. As she goes through the motions of the prep, Harris's only thought is of that drug.

Once all is prepared and loaded into that same dirty needle, she's been using on him since the day he called himself coming to bring her back home to him. She retrieves a stand-alone mirror from the other room and sets it in front of him. This is the first time he's seen himself since he arrived. He's taken aback and nearly brought to tears by the sight of what he's become at the hands of his once feeble wife. She violently rips the duct tape from his mouth.

"Ow, fuck, Chels! I should kick your ass!"

"I would love to see you try." She laughs wickedly loud.

"Why don't you just get it over and kill me?" he says, looking at his pathetic image.

"Awe, are you starting to feel like you

should have kept your ass in Detroit? You wanted me back so bad that you thought you could intimidate me to go back to that hell hole of a life with you. The hurt and pain that you inflicted on me for all those years are going to be dished out to you until I'm tired of it. I don't appreciate what you've done to Brooklyn and don't even try to lie and say that you didn't do anything to her because you left your fucking calling card on her flesh. You are so fucking vain; you just have to carve your name into everything that you touch."

"Yeah, I kicked her ass, and I told her I would if I found out that she lied about where you were. And I'm going to do the same to you when I get out of this chair." He says, wiggling around trying to free himself."

"Well, I hope you don't think that I'm going to help get loose." She laughs again before taking another drag of her cigarette, then with all her might she knocks him to the floor, causing him to hit his head on the wall.
He sees that she clearly isn't the same meek, frail, apologetic and forgiving woman he married, and it isn't just her actions that make him wonder, it is the way she carries herself and the tone that she takes with him not to mention the smoking.

She fills the syringe to 5 ccs, taps out the air bubbles and finds a vein. She withdraws a bit of blood to check for a good flow...it's Good. Slowly, she presses the plunger injecting the burning concoction into his veins. He's used to the burn and, he feels relief from the pains of the infected parts of his body where the drug has damaged his flesh to a deep black scaly scar of gangrene with greenish pus seeping through the scabs.

She makes herself comfortable in front of him and watches the effects of the drug as his head begins to nod while he mumbles gibberish that only he can understand.

"That a boy...you fuck! Soak it all in. I am soon done with you."

ENOUGH IS ENOUGH
THREE MONTHS LATER

It's six-thirty in the evening and completely dark outside as Brooklyn walks home from the grocery store when she hears someone behind her whispering, "That's her. Let's get her!" She sees a tall manly figure approaching her and increases her pace towards him, passing her apartment building.

"Excuse me, sir." She says to the stranger, still unable to see his face.

"Yes?" he replies, bringing his face closer to hers.

"Oh my God, no!" she screams.
Two men behind her run up and begin to beat her with an aluminum bat. The man she asked to help stands by and watches the attack without attempting to help her at all. It isn't long before her screams are silent and she is left for dead, lying in a pool of her blood.
Brooklyn wakes up, screaming and sweating. She is grateful it was only a dream...a dream that seems to repeat itself every night, but reveals a little more detail than the night before.

***

January 23rd, three months after the police cleared Ron's house to him after the shooting investigation, Brooklyn's condition has improved enough for her to be released from the hospital but with assistance for getting around. She also sees a speech therapist twice a week. Ron has popped the question, and they are closer than ever. Chelsea usually stays at his house to spend time with him instead of taking the chance of him hearing Harris moving around upstairs.

Ron has since given Chelsea the Bouvier to protect her when she does stay at home. The dog has grown quite a bit, no longer looking like a puppy but more like the size of a horse. Every time she allows the dog in the house, she runs straight to the door that leads upstairs, sniffing around the bottom of it and scratching at it. Chelsea has become nose-blind to the stench near the door. However, when she opens it, the stench hits her like a ton of bricks. She has invested in a box of medical facemasks.

    On this particular day when the dog runs into the bedroom, scratching and stiffing at the upstairs door, Chelsea decides that it's time to do something with Harris. After feeding the dog and sending her back outside, she retrieves the key to the upstairs door and puts on the medical mask.

    As she walks into the room, Harris is slumped over in the chair that he has been bound to since her last injection to him. His pants have crusted over with urine and feces.

The skin on his neck and arms has turned black and peeling away from the flesh. A portion of his neck where she has been injecting him has ulcerated with greenish-yellow pus oozing out of the injected areas of his body. His skin is peeling away, exposing the flesh of his muscles and fat. His speech and motor skill have declined terribly. Sporadically he will say things that can be understood, but it is hardly relevant to her, the rest of the time he's mostly growling or moaning with his mouth ajar.

"Chels, what the fuck are you pumping into my body?" He slurs.

"Why? Are you not enjoying the rides?"

"I'm in serious pain. I think I need to go to the hospital."

"Ha! You are funny. You need to go to the hospital!" she says loudly with a genuine laugh. "Do you mean like when I needed to go to the hospital when you hung me from the basement ceiling for days while I was pregnant? Is that the kind of hospital you're talking about? Because as I remember it, instead of you taking me to the hospital, you brought your doctor friend over to treat me and made him swear to keep it all under wraps. So, if that's the kind of hospital you need, then I can certainly accommodate you, jack ass!" She replies in a deep maniacal laughter.

"But something is terribly wrong. Do you

see what's happening to my skin?"

"Well, yes, I do!" She replies with admiration. "I love the way this stuff works. I don't think I could have come up with better karmic action than this. No need to worry about what's happening to your flesh, it's only gangrene, it'll all fall off soon."

The stench of the chemicals cooking causes him to have withdrawal effects, and he begins to beg for the drug.

"Oh, shit!" He blurts out from frustration as she teases him with the drug, pretending to give it to him but then takes it back.

"Why don't you just kill me, Chels? It's a lot simpler."

"Well, there are a couple of reasons why I won't kill you, and the first one is you're not worth me going to jail for the rest of my life. The second reason is, if you die without experiencing the shit you inflicted on people, you'll only be reincarnated to commit the same evil in your second life. Therefore, you should be grateful that I'm helping you to be a better person in your next life. That's if you believe in that kind of shit." She giggles.

She slowly pushes the plunger...he moans in pain as the chemicals still burn as it travels through his veins. As the effects of the drug reach his brain, his body rocks back and forth, his mouth ajar and he begins to moan gutturally, sounding animal-like.

"There you go. See, the hospital won't make you feel like that. Now, don't you feel better, prick?"

"Uhhaa." He moans as it is the only thing he can muster until the drug wears off.

"I'll be back in an hour to give you more." She assures him before leaving the room, closing the door behind her. As she descends the stairs, she realizes that she's bored with him now and is ready to pick up where she left off before he came to get her.

"I need this to go over smoothly and without incident. He has to be a willing participant that doesn't make a scene when I dispose of him." She silently thinks with a maniacal grin growing upon her face as she locks the door behind her.

The telephone rings when she enters the dining room.

"Hello?" she answers.

"Chels?"

"Hey, Brook, I was going to call to see if you wanted company."

"Um...I would be...fun too."

"Happy... you would be happy too?"

"Yes."

"I can tell that speech therapy is really helping. I'm so proud of you."

"Me too." Brooklyn smiles inside.

"Good. You should be. I was thinking of bringing a game to play if you're up to a little company."

"Yes…bu-but not too hard to know."

"Too hard to play; you mean?"

"Yes. Come. I made food."

"Okay, I'll stop and get something for dessert and bring the Othello game."

"Yay!"

"See you soon, Brook."

"Bye, bye.'

*

After three games of Othello; for the tiebreaker, dinner, and dessert, it has become later than Chelsea thought it would as she and Brook grow sleepy.

"Well, I guess I'll head home since it's gotten so late."

"Chels, please!"

"What?" Chelsea responds, genuinely concerned.

"Stay!"

"Sure; are you okay?"

"I see his face all night!" Brook replies with tears filling her eyes.

"Who's face?"

"The one that…hits me."

"You mean, you have bad dreams about him?"

"All the time." she nods. "I think he knows

who I am...in the b-bat dre-dream. In my b-bat dream, I know him, but I don't know if the dre-dream is only a dream. I cannot know...the real." Brooklyn explains as she struggles for the correct words.

"You are safe now Brook, and I will stay here with you as long as you like, but I am pretty certain that you don't have to worry about that person anymore."

"Huh? Is he found?"

"I'm sure that the police are right on his trail. You're safe." Chelsea assures.

"I don't feel so."

"Do you trust me?" Chelsea asks.

"Of course."

"Then believe me when I say, you are safe."

3:02 a.m.

Chelsea is awakened to an annoying persistent sound. Slowly she opens her eyes as she looks around in the dark, the sound is more profound, sounding like an injured puppy and for a moment she thinks she's at home and that her dog is whimpering. She sets up in bed and turns on the lamp beside the bed, rubs her eyes and looks around again.

"Fuck that bitch up! I told you if I found out that you knew where she was, that I was going to make you pay." A man yells in Brooklyn's face as she is led down the street past her apartment by

two large men. She struggles to get away, yelling and screaming for help before an excruciating pain to her head causes everything to go black.
She sees herself in the back seat of a car appearing to be asleep, but as she looks upon herself, she senses something very wrong as she feels the car in motion.
Desperately, she yells at herself.
"Get up! Come on! Get up and jump out of the car. Come on, please!"
As she grabs herself by the shoulders to shake herself awake, she is sunken into herself, still mentally trying to wake up."

Chelsea follows the sound to the light of Brooklyn's bedroom where she sees Brook lying in the fetal position, whimpering and stiff as a board.

"Brook wake up honey," Chelsea calls out. She approaches the bedside, but still no movement, only whimpering.

"Wake up, Brook, you're dreaming." She says, shaking her by the shoulders to wake her.

"Wake up!" Brook yells at herself with a nudge to her shoulder. "Open the door and jump out! Open your eyes!"

"Brook, wake up, you're dreaming." Chelsea continues to shake her.

The more she tries to open her eyes, the harder it is to keep them open. The more she struggles to wake up, the deeper her fear grows as her gut feeling tells her that she is going to die. She wants so much to wake up, and it all just is a dream but, she can't move, and her screams go unheard as she cannot seem to scream any louder than inside her closed mouth. Her eyes open for only a second but, her eyelids are so heavy that she can't keep them open, making her fall right back into the terror she's experiencing.

"Come on, Brook! It's just a dream…wake up."

Again, her eyes open and shut. She can barely breathe as is sucked right back into the horror. *"Get up!" Brooklyn yells at herself one more time as she forces herself to move an arm or leg…even a finger, something, movement to fully wake her up, but her body is so heavy that she can't seem to make the simplest motion of her limbs.*

"Brook?" Chelsea calls as she taps her face lightly. "Wake up. Everything is ok." She assures her as she sees her eyes opening and closing. "Come on."

Finally, she can move her hand and touch the car door and open it, and with all her might, she jumps out of the moving car landing on the concrete.

Brook wakes with a start nearly falling out of the bed as Chelsea is still tapping her on the cheek.

"It's ok. You were having a nightmare."
"Oh! He's evil!"
"Who is evil? What happened?"
"He hit me," Brooklyn replies trembling all over and still frightened.
"Your attacker?"
"Yes. He knows me…I think I know him too. I know, I know, I-I know, I-I know." Brook begins to cry.
"It's ok," Chelsea replies with hugs, trying to sooth her trembling friend. "You are safe, and I am here with you. It's all ok."
"But…I-I-know," she cries on Chelsea's shoulder.
"It's alright now. I'm going to make you something hot to drink. What would you like? Tea? Hot chocolate?"
"Don't leave me. I don't want to sleep."
"Do you want to watch television?"
"Ok."
"Do you want to watch it in bed or in the living room?"
"Here," Brooklyn replies as she taps the space beside her on the bed.
"No problem."
"You welcome?" Brook says.
"You mean, "thank you.""
"Uhmm, hmm."
Chelsea gets under the blankets with Brook and hands her the television remote. She takes the

remote with trembling hands.

"Brook, do you want to talk about it? I mean, do you want to tell me about your dream?"

"Uhm, uhm…I can't know, is it a picture or did it happen?

"You mean, you don't know if it's a dream or not?"

"Yeah."

"Tell me what happened."

"The man is uhm…evil. He is uhm, uhm mad for me."

"For what?"

"I uhm…uhm say something, he uhm not like, I think."

"You said something to make him mad at you? What did you say?"

"I don't uhm know. He told me to pay for uhm…uhm…I can't realize."

"You mean, you can't remember?"

"uhm hmm. Re-rem-ember. I'm sca-scared, so they hit me, and I am in black in a car. I can't know where it's going, and I can't wake up. Feel…I feel like uhm…I'm dying and won't wake up. I scream and scream, and I won't wake." Brook recalls the dream with tears pooling in her eyes.

"It's okay Brook," Chelsea says with a hug. "You are safe, and it was only a bad dream."

"No…no! Is why I speech this way! It's not a

dream! I know the man's look. I have to know him!"

"Why do you think that you know who this person is?"

"Because I have to pay."

"Pay for what Brook? What did you pay for? Was it in the dream that you paid for something?"

"No, something else; something I can't re-mem-ber!" She replies with frustration.

"Ok, ok. Let's calm down. Have you told your therapist about your dreams?"

"Yeah." She replies as she reaches for a journal she keeps in the drawer of her nightstand. "I write it."

"Your therapist told you to write your dreams in this book? Did she say why?"

"They can't be the same, so I should write it to help uhm...my uhm mem-memory?"

"Ok. I understand. Does it seem to work?"

"I think, yes, because I know him now."

"May I read it?"

"You can try," Brooklyn says as she hands the book to her.

"Why do you say I 'can try'?"

"I'm uhm not good at pencil anymore." Awake until daybreak, Chelsea reads as much as she can with understanding while Brooklyn attempts to translate, and for every hand gesture, she makes to explain her writings a scar almost identical to the scars Chelsea bares on her own body reawakens something vengeful in her. She hides her fury well as one of her personalities emerges without Brooklyn noticing.

"I know you said that killing the fucker would cause problems for Chelsea but, in actuality when he recovers don't think the shit-stain will come back for her?" Says personality Julia. "Something has to be done, and it needs to be done soon."

"If anything is done, it can't lead back to us." Replies Billie.

"Trust me...it won't." Julia says.

"Ch-Chelsea?" Brooklyn calls out, keeping Julia present.

"Brook, I hope you know that whoever has caused this trauma to you, will pay for what they've done to you and anyone else they may have caused harm to."

"No...I pay for because I can't re-know who he is."

"I know that you can't remember, and you may not have to remember because Karma is a bitch and she is sure to come back around and when she does duck because she hits hard."

"Ka-karma? Who is she?"

"She's your best friend. She may not come when you want her, but when she does...look out."

EVERY DOG HAS IT'S DAY
DEVIL'S BREATH

Brooklyn eventually falls asleep an hour later, but the personalities that came through remained awake until the break of day, contemplating the best way to handle Harris.

"Brook?"

Chelsea's alter calls as she shakes Brooklyn by the shoulder.

"Mmm?"

"Brook, I have to go, but I've made you some tea and a bit of breakfast."

"Oh, thank you." She replies as she groggily awakes.

"How do you feel?"

"Good?" She replies before taking a sip of the tea.

"Good is wonderful. You finally fell asleep, and that's even better."

"Sorry, Chels."

"For what?"

"You to stay awake for me."

"Hey, I will always be here for you. You can call me any time, and I will be here. I'm just glad you were able to go back to sleep after your nightmare. I'm sorry for falling asleep on you. I guess I just couldn't keep my eyes open any longer."

"I don't know if you sleep. I-I-I was, uhm...so...sc-scary. I not shut my eyes ever."

"I completely understand, I've had plenty of scary dreams myself."

"Yes?"

"Yes. I must go now; do you think you'll be alright? Do you need anything before I go?"

"I can be alright now," Brooklyn replies. "Thank you."

"Any time. I'll call and check on you later, okay?"

"Okay."

**

Once in the car, Chelsea begins to resurface as Julia fades into the background with a sounding last thought of *"enough is enough"* in their minds.

Before going home, she stops by to see Ron. She lets herself into his house and finds him grabbing his car keys.

"Well, what a pleasant surprise!" He says.

"Good afternoon. I guess I should have called first. I see you're on your way out."

"Hmm," he scoffs. "I was getting ready to go visit you but, here you are in front of me. What brings you by?"

"Probably the same reason you were going to visit me."

"Oh?"

"Yes, I miss you." She replies with a sweet kiss to his luscious lips.

"Mmm, with kisses like that, I know I miss you."

"So, seriously, where were you going?"

"Seriously, I was going to run some errands and then stop by to visit with you, then maybe persuade you to let me stay the night with you." He replies, embracing her.

"You know you don't need to persuade me. That invitation is always open but, if you rather persuade me, I'd like to see what you got. Although I'd rather stay the night here with you."

"That's fine with me babe, just as long as I get to wake up with you next to me...more importantly spending quality time with you. Do you want to go out tonight or just chill here with a movie?"

"Whatever we decide, I'm looking forward to it." She replies. "I just need to run some errands myself."

"Ok. How about we meet up around dinner?"

"That sounds like a good time. I may make a stop and see Brooklyn before heading back this way if that's alright with you."

"Oh, of course. How is she doing these days?"

"Every day is a challenge for her but, she's getting better at communicating and seeing her therapist less, now that she's getting better."

"Is she still seeing that guy, Morgan?"

"She is; he's just away on travel. I think she said he should be back soon."

"Well, I'm glad he hung around through all of this. I know it's got to be a lot to take in so early in their relationship, but it does prove how much he really cares for her."

"Yeah, I think we are the luckiest girls." She replies with another kiss.

He kisses her passionately as he caresses down her back and around her hips.

"I better go take care of these errands before we end up in bed and not getting anything done." He whispers in her ear, leaving a smile on her face with her eyes still closed from the kiss.

"Yes, you're right. I'll see you tonight around 6:30 or so." She says as she walks out with him following closely behind her.

"See you then, sweetheart."

***

Chelsea pulls into the driveway, and as soon as the dog hears the gravel crunching beneath the car tires and runs out of her dog house barking and jumping around.

"Hey, pretty girl!" She calls out to the dog.

"Hey, Kizzy! I'm sorry for leaving you alone last night."

She heads straight for the dog with hugs and kisses then releases her from her chains before refreshing the dog's water tub. While the dog runs around the yard stretching her legs, Chelsea goes into the house and prepares a nice warm treat of leftovers simmering on the stove while she packs an overnight bag. She hears the dog barking and scratching at the door.

"Alright, Kizzy. I know you smell the food." She says on her way back to the kitchen to allow the dog in the house. She mixes the heated leftovers with the dogfood and bangs on the dish while calling for the dog but, as usual, the dog is in the bedroom where she's sniffing around the bottom of the upstairs door and scratching the door to gain access.

"Kizzy! Come on, girl! Come and eat!" She calls out as she opens the back door and carries the food to the doghouse with the dog following her. She chains the dog to the house, and goes back into the house, grabs her overnight bag.

As she approaches the bedroom, her alter personalities are reflecting in the vanity mirror with an unrelenting expression, summoning her to come closer. Gradually, their voices become clearer and aggressive as they debate over what to do with Harris.

"It's time for him to go. I don't care how, but

you have to get him out of the house and soon." The calm one says.

"I agree," Julia says. *"But you know that he will come back for you, and he maybe just foolish enough to try to kill you if you don't fix it so that he can't come back."*

"I've never harmed anyone in my whole life," Chelsea responds.

"Well, its time that you do." Julia says, taking a pull on her cigarette.

"I hate to say it, but she's right." **The calm one speaks again.** *"It's either him or you. What do you want to do? Do you want to take that chance and risk him coming back to abuse you again or worst...kill you? Has he not done enough to make you fear for your life? Even after causing the death of the baby?"*

She enters the room and takes a seat at the vanity completely focused on the reflections she sees in the mirror as if she no longer has free will. She reaches under the vanity table, and as if controlled by some entity, without taking her eyes off the mirror, she retrieves a cigarette from a pack that is taped to the underside of the vanity and lights it. Gradually, Chelsea's voice disappears in the distance as the discussion of what to do next is taken over by Julia.

"Here is what's going to happen, and it has to happen tonight. This house needs to be cleaned and cleaned well. He will be willing and obedient.

Chelsea needs to cancel her evening with Ron. There is no room for error."

***

"Ron, I'm going to have to cancel tonight. I'm so sorry."

"What's going on? Do you want me to come to you instead?"

"No, sweetie, thank you. It's Brook, she's afraid to be alone tonight. She's been having horrible nightmares of her attack, and she doesn't want to be alone."

"Well, you know I have the extra room, and she's more than welcome to sleep here."

"You are such a sweetheart." She says. "The problem is that she's afraid to sleep alone. She falls into these deep night terrors, and it's hard for her to wake up. The other night I stayed with her, and I could hear her from the guest room moaning in fear. She was so grateful that I was there to wake her from the dream."

"Jesus, that sounds horrible! I know, and I'm so sorry to cancel on you but, know that I do miss lying next to you wrapped in your arms."

"Well, just let me know if you or she needs anything. I am here for you, and I love you."

"I love you too...so very much, I love you."

"You owe me big time, you know." He jokes.

"And I'm happy to pay in full. I'll keep you posted on things. She's actually doing so much better than before. She at least feels safe in her own home now, when before it was a challenge."

"I understand and can only imagine the horror she's been through, not to mention being haunted by the whole incident."

"I really appreciate your patience, Ron. I really do."

"Of course! Who am I to come between your lifelong friendship with her? It's a rare thing to have someone friends as long as you have, not to mention the fact that the relationship between you two is so strong. I wish I had something as solid as the two of you."

"You do."

"Oh?"

"You have me."

"You're sweet. Maybe we can spend some time together tomorrow, and since Morgan is out of town on business, we can include Brooklyn."

"That sounds nice Ron."

"Of course, I think it would help to have her engage in everyday activities outside of her therapy and doctor's appointments. Maybe it will leave more pleasant images in her mind to dream about than that night."

"I don't know why I didn't think of that. I guess I was just so upset and hurt over what happened to her that even I have been focused on catching the degenerates who did this to her than giving her something more pleasant to think about."

"Sometimes, you have to step out of the circle to get a clear picture of what would be more helpful than actually being emotionally involved. But it only makes sense that you are emotionally involved, as you are.
I would be the same if it were you that this happened to. My only thought would be to kill whoever was responsible for harming you, and nothing else."

"I'm glad I have you to help me through this, and I will definitely suggest to Brook that the three of us do something together."

"Wonderful. I look forward to it."

"I love you, Ron." She says.

"And you know that I love you. I hope to hear from tomorrow."

"You will...whether you want to or not." She laughs.

"Goodnight, sweetheart."

"Goodnight." She replies before hanging up.

***

Chelsea unlocks the door to the upstairs, and as usual, she closes the door and locks it behind her. As she ascends the stairs, her fear of him grows. Gradually her alter personality Julia comes to the surface and with her, a fury Chelsea could never display towards Harris, despite all that he has done to her. As Chelsea fades into Julia, her now faint voice screams out, "be careful."

She unlocks the door, and the odor of dank urine and feces emanates in the room. Quickly she grabs a surgical mask and puts it on.

"Oh, my God! You smell like shit!"

"What do you expect, Chelsea? It's not like you allow me to relieve myself properly."

"Well, you don't have to worry about that anymore buddy, because it's time for you to go."

Fear sets in as he feels his life in her hands and what is to come of this horrible ordeal.

"Look; I'll make a deal with you," Harris says. "If you let me go, I swear I won't turn to the police. I will forget about all of this and move on."

"Ah, for real?" She replies with hopeful eyes and praying hands.

"Absolutely!"

"And will you go away and forever leave me alone too?"

"Of course. I shouldn't have come out here for you in the first place."

"Well, no shit, Sherlock! You couldn't just leave well enough alone. You had to prove to yourself how fucking big your balls really are by intimidating and paying a couple of underpaid cowardice cops to try and take out my friends and keep eyes on me. And for what? You thought you were coming to get ole Chelsea and drag her

back home with you and pick up where you left off, with her being your punching bag and toy."

"I'm sorry. I don't know what I was thinking."

"Well, it's nice to finally hear you apologize for something but, I know that apology is not for me but, for you. You're probably sorry as hell that you set foot in Virginia, let alone my front step." She says as she mixes his next hit and prepares it for injection. "You would never apologize for the life you took from us, of your own flesh and blood. You hadn't even asked about the baby since you've set foot in this house, you heartless piece of shit. Maybe you did us a favor in that fact. You spared us from being reminded of you."

"Who is this 'us' you keep speaking of?" he asks, as he begins to hurt for the drug that she's mixing.

"None of your fucking business. You don't matter anymore, and this is your last hit from me." She says, as she tightens the tourniquet around his arm and taps for a vein and injects him. "Now, on this flight, you should focus on all the evil you are and have inflicted on others, including, the victims of all of your clients. That dirty ass doctor you had to come to check on me, and the fucking pedophiles that you knew were guilty and getting them off scot-free. Yeess, enjoy your ride of pride...the pride you took in hurting so many and your unborn child." She says as if she is a flight attendant.

While Harris fades into a krokodile high Chelsea's alter begins to clean and bag all of the drug paraphernalia until it's time to dispose of it. She scrubs the floor where Harris urinated on himself for so long. The stench of it all to too strong for the surgical mask as it penetrates it. She opens the windows to allow some of the cleaning solutions and odor to air out.

She goes downstairs and into the kitchen where she places the drug paraphernalia in a Ziploc bag goes to her grandfather's bedroom closet where she stashed Harris' jacket the night he arrived and puts the drugs in the inside chest pocket.

"This jacket has to go with him, so it's better if the drugs are found on him." She says out loud as if someone is listening. *"Doesn't look like it fits him anymore."* She says in another tone of voice. *"Doesn't matter. Everything that he touched and came here with has to be disposed of with him. This house a clean sweep before our final move so, double check the stairs to make sure nothing fell out of his pockets when we drug him up there."*

**

It's 8:30 in the evening by the time all the cleaning is complete. Before returning upstairs, Chelsea's alter personality Julia, returns to the kitchen and retrieve a large trash bag and covers the car seat where he'll be sitting. On her way back into the house, she grabs a pair of latex gloves from under the sink. She unlocks the door and heads upstairs. She finds that it is as cold as it is outside and well aired out. There is still a bit of odor but, not as bad as before.

"Fuck it's cold up here!" she exclaims on her way up the stairs, as she remembers leaving the windows open. *"He must be cold,"* Chelsea says in the faint distance of their minds. *"Why the fuck do you care?"* Julia asks.

"Who are you talking to?" Harris asks, as he gradually comes down from his high.

"None of your damn business." She replies.

"Well, fuck you then bitch!" he snaps.

"We'll see whose getting fucked this time around."

She puts on a pair of latex gloves and retrieves the package that officer Vadal had left for her. She opens the wrapper revealing a small amount of an off-white, grayish powder and blows the powder into Harris's face. Taken aback, he shakes his head from side to side to shake off the powdered drug but, it's too late, he has inhaled it and is now taking effect.

"Now, I want you to behave yourself and act like you have home training because I'm about to release you."

"You are?" he asks.

"Yes, but what are you going to do?" she asks.

"I'm going to act like I have home training." He replies innocently.

"*Good boy.*"

She leads him down the stairs and instructs him to put on his jacket before leading him out the back door to seat him on the trash bag covered seat of the car.

He's compliant and pleasant, and even if he wanted to put up a fight, he can't. The drug she blew into his face renders him to her will. Whatever she asks or tells him to do, he will without question. He's as helpless as an innocent child.

It's nearly 10:00 in the evening by the time they arrive in D.C. As Chelsea's alter, Julia, drives along McPherson square, there is a sea of invisible people lying on the sidewalks and benches of the street with their every possession close to them or being pushed in a shopping cart. Many are sleeping under cardboard boxes or tents as the temperatures drop. She comes to a stop light and looks around.

"*There is a bag in your pocket with a needle in it.*" She says.

"It is?"

"*Yes. Take it out and look at it.*"

Without question, he removes the bag and finds the syringe with the drug already in it and ready to be used.

"Now I want you to get out of the car and go over to the bench where that man is laying." She instructs as she tightens the tourniquet at his wrist. *"I need you to take a seat on the ground next to that man and inject all of the medicine in this needle into the vein in your hand. Do you understand what I said?"*

"Yes. I'm going to sit over there and give myself this medicine in this vein of my hand." He replies without concern.

"Very good. Now get out and do what I told you to do."

Harris gets out of the car and almost immediately blends end with the homeless people around him, with his tattered clothes, body odor, urine and feces caked on to his pants. He takes a seat on the ground beside the bench and injects the full amount of the syringe into his vein. She watched him slump against the bench then drove off.

***

Three days later, Chelsea is sitting in the Livingroom watching television while visiting Brooklyn, who is in the kitchen pouring a glass of milk to take her medication with. She is puzzled by the missing person's picture on the carton. He looks familiar to her, and yet, she can't place who he is or where she may know him from.

"A body was found this morning beside a

bench here on McPherson among the homeless people of D.C.," says the news reporter.

Chelsea is saddened by the news of the poor people of D.C. and that they don't seem to have family that they can turn to.

"It appears it may have been a drug overdose, as a syringe was still sticking out of his vein but, we won't know for sure until after an autopsy. The person was barefoot and without a coat or jacket. It's possible he could have been robbed of those things before he passed. The police are asking for your help with this case and would like you to call the non-emergency number with any information."

As Chelsea continues to watch the news report, she gradually fades into the distance of her mind as Julia resurfaces, putting a maniacal grin upon her face as she's confident that the person being reported on is Chelsea's husband.

"There. See, you never have to worry about that fucker anymore. Never to return. And for all the dirt he's done, no one is going to be looking for him." Julia says, with a deep sigh and joyful smile.

"Until death do, we part." Chelsea says under her breath as Julia fades into the background.

The End

Copyright © 2009 S. L. Carter
All rights reserved.

Made in the USA
Middletown, DE
26 January 2020